"I didn[illegible] been [illegible] calf wr[illegible] helping Sammy," Morgan admitted.

Jolie blinked. Had she heard him right?

"I came to tell you that I'll do whatever I need to do to help you help him," Morgan continued. His amazing blue eyes softened—he was actually conceding.

"G-good," Jolie stammered. As she looked at him, she thought about trying to apologize again, telling him that she hadn't meant to hurt him. But she knew he would only deny that she'd hurt him in the first place. "That's the way it should be. Our past, what happened between us—"

"Is the past," he said, firmly.

"Yes. We should still be able to help these boys even though we once had feelings for each other and it didn't work out."

What else could she say? She'd just come up against one wall after the other with him; he'd made it clear there was no sense in rehashing old [illegible] e to revisit. So she [illegible]

For [illegible]

Books by Debra Clopton

Love Inspired

The Trouble with Lacy Brown
And Baby Makes Five
No Place Like Home
Dream a Little Dream
Meeting Her Match
Operation: Married by Christmas
Next Door Daddy
Her Baby Dreams
The Cowboy Takes a Bride
Texas Ranger Dad
Small-Town Brides
"A Mule Hollow Match"
Lone Star Cinderella
His Cowgirl Bride
†Her Forever Cowboy
†Cowboy for Keeps
Yukon Cowboy
†Yuletide Cowboy
Small-Town Moms
"A Mother for Mule Hollow"
**Her Rodeo Cowboy
**Her Lone Star Cowboy
**Her Homecoming Cowboy
††Her Unforgettable Cowboy

*Mule Hollow
†Men of Mule Hollow
**Mule Hollow Homecoming
††Cowboys of Sunrise Ranch

DEBRA CLOPTON

First published in 2005, Debra Clopton is an award-winning multipublished novelist who has won a Booksellers Best Award, an Inspirational Readers' Choice Award, a Golden Quill, a *Cataromance* Reviewers' Choice Award, *RT Book Reviews* Book of the Year and Harlequin.com's Readers' Choice Award. She was also a 2004 finalist in the prestigious RWA Golden Heart, a triple finalist in the American Christian Fiction Writers Carol Award and most recently a finalist in the 2011 Gayle Wilson Award for Excellence.

Married for twenty-two blessed years to her high school sweetheart, Debra was widowed in 2003. Happily, in 2008, a couple of friends played matchmaker and set her up on a blind date. Instantly hitting it off, they were married in 2010. They live in the country with her husband's two high-school-age sons. Debra has two adult sons, a lovely daughter-in-law and a beautiful granddaughter—life is good! Her greatest awards are her family and spending time with them. You can reach Debra at P.O. Box 1125, Madisonville, TX 77864 or at debraclopton.com.

Her Unforgettable Cowboy

Debra Clopton

Recycling programs for this product may not exist in your area.

ISBN-13: 978-0-373-87811-6

HER UNFORGETTABLE COWBOY

This edition published by arrangement with Love Inspired Books.

www.LoveInspiredBooks.com

Printed in U.S.A.

I will not leave you as orphans—I will come for you.

—*John* 14:18

In memory of Ms. Jo,
Grandma Edith and Grandma Sylvia.
Thinking of each of you makes me smile.

Special thanks goes to Carolyn and Joyce for the research trip to The Purple Cow—what a fun day we had. I think you'll see the research paid off well.

Also a big thank-you to my editor, Melissa Endlich—your insights and encouragement in this new venture were spot on.

Chapter One

Sunrise Ranch, Dew Drop, Texas

"Calm down, son."

Morgan McDermott's father, Randolph, cut Morgan off at the pass with a rasp of exasperation—which in no way, shape or form even began to match the anger-fueled exasperation Morgan was struggling to contain.

An imposing figure at fifty-two, Randolph had hair as black as the Texas oil pumping from the herd of wells across the ten-thousand-acre McDermott family ranch. The only differences between the two men—who shared chiseled high cheekbones and square-jawed features—was the whisper of white at Randolph's temples and twenty years. Randolph was as physically fit and hard-headed as any of his three sons.

"Calm down?" Morgan gave a harsh laugh. "Are you kidding me? You go behind my back and hire my *ex*-fiancée, and you expect me to calm down? For starters, Dad, we're partners. I'm supposed to make decisions like this *with* you. Second..."

Morgan was so shaken up by what he'd just been told that he lost his train of thought.

Jolie Sheridan, here.

Randolph pushed back from his desk and rose, meeting Morgan eye to eye. "You know as well as I do that we needed a teacher and we needed one quick. Jolie has graciously agreed to fill the position for one semester—"

"I don't care if *she's* paying *you* to let her teach the boys here at the ranch—I don't want her here." Morgan would never use this tone with his father under normal circumstances. But being blindsided by the knowledge that his dad had gone behind his back and hired the woman who had broken his heart was not normal circumstances. "We're supposed to discuss this kind of thing, Dad."

"I understand your feelings, but there was no time. Besides, Jolie is familiar with the school and will fit right in."

Logically it made sense, but that didn't ease the betrayal. Morgan remained silent, trying to grasp the reality of his situation.

"Your past is something I'd hoped you'd overcome by now. I hated that you got hurt when she left. We all did. That said, I've made a decision and it stands."

Morgan rammed a hand through his hair. "How do you expect me to—" He halted at the stern look his dad shot him.

"I expect you to act like a man, not a brokenhearted teenager nursing a grudge."

His dad's words stung. "I got over her a long time ago and you know it," he growled, not remembering the last time—if ever—that he'd been this angry with his father.

"Did you?" Randolph studied him, unflinching, from across the wide oak desk.

"You know I did. That doesn't mean I want to be around her for the next four months."

"You're strong. You'll make it. Maybe God worked the details out so you can come to some kind of peace with the situation. You may have gotten over Jolie, but you haven't forgiven her. You can't have peace until you do that."

This was a no-win situation. Yanking a noose tight around his emotions Morgan snatched his hat from the hat rack. "I'm late," he said, turning to leave. He pushed open the door of the Sunrise Ranch offices, his father's words trailing him.

"Mind your manners, Morgan McDermott. And remember, those boys out there are watching every move you make and learning from you."

"Some partnership," Morgan growled as the blazing Texas heat hit him full force. It didn't begin to compare to the sizzling heat of his fury.

His life had just turned into a train wreck.

Ramming his hat onto his head, Morgan battled to get a grip on his anger. Stalking across fifty yards of white-rock gravel separating the barns from the office and chow hall, he fought to rein in his emotions. He had a herd of boys enjoying a very special moment in the barn and he intended to be a part of it come baseball-size hail or high water. And he knew—without his dad reminding him—that they didn't need to see him furious.

Sunrise Ranch was a working cattle ranch and foster home for boys who needed stability in their lives. Morgan took his job as their protector and role model extremely seriously. If he didn't, he wouldn't still be on the ranch in the first place.

Despite the heat or Morgan's mood, excitement rang in the early-morning air hanging over the ranch compound. Quickening his stride, Morgan approached the sun-faded red stable, the birthplace of hundreds of foals over the years. The sturdy, low-slung building had been on the property since Morgan's great-great-grandfather built it back in the early 1900s. Through the years there had been new barns and buildings added, but this lovingly maintained stable and the other historic buildings that dotted the property carried the memories of those who'd been here before him. This was their legacy to him and his two brothers, Rowdy and Tucker. His family took to heart the responsibility of passing it on to future generations.

Morgan hauled in a deep breath the moment he stepped through the stable's double doors. Instantly the scent of grassy, sundried hay and feed mingled with the smell of leather and horses, filled his lungs. And his spirit.

The stables held lots of memories from years gone by, but it was the hushed whispers of the boys at the end of the building that filled his soul and gave his life purpose.

Before his mother's death when he was eleven years old, Lydia McDermott had had a vision to share the beauty and blessing of their West Texas ranch with less fortunate boys who had no place to call home. She'd died before she could make her dream a reality, but Morgan's dad and grandmother worked tirelessly over the next two years, getting the ranch approved as a foster home.

For the last eighteen years, sixteen boys at a time had made Sunrise Ranch their home. And Morgan, who had become a full partner six months ago, intended to help carry the torch forward—no matter who his dad brought on as the boys' teacher.

Moving down the concrete alley, the clink of his spurs and scuff of his boots bounced off the stalls. The chatter halted from the huddle at the end where a new colt had just been born, and the boys who were new to the ranch turned, awe on their faces. There was nothing like watching the miracle of life.

Yup, that was the only reminder Morgan needed that the boys came first.

Striding to stand behind them, Morgan patted one of the newcomers on the back and looked at the foal.

"It's about time you dragged yourself out here to take a look at the new little filly," Walter Pepper, his horse foreman, teased from inside the stall where he'd been assisting the mother. One of the best horsemen around, Pepper—as he'd been tagged in his early years—had worked at the ranch since he was a teenager, hired on by Morgan's granddad forty-five years ago. A stocky cowboy with a white head of hair, a gruff voice and a heart of gold, he loved to tease.

Taking in the coal-black filly curled up in the soft hay beside his momma, Morgan gave a crooked smile. "Looks like y'all've got it under control."

"She's as black as *your* hair, Morgan," nine-year-old Caleb declared, his green eyes shining. A blond-headed creative thinker and doer, Caleb was a regular fixer-upper, always coming up with ideas and taking tools and machines apart in the shop to figure out how they worked. But right now, he was wide-eyed like the rest of them, watching the mother horse tend to her newborn baby.

"Yeah," B.J. said, a grin lifting the seven-year-old's plump cheeks. "She ain't got no streak a white in her black hair like Beauty or Mr. Randolph gots." He puffed out his chest, proud that he was the first to make the comparison between the jet-black horse with the white lightning bolt crossing her face, and Randolph and his white temples.

"You're right about that, son," Morgan agreed, tousling B.J.'s brown hair as he studied Beauty. She was the first of twenty-five mares on the ranch who were due to foal in the next two months and she was kicking off the season like a pro. When the baby unbuckled her long legs and tried to stand, Beauty began nudging her gently on the rump, encouraging her as she struggled to gain her wobbly legs.

"Look, fellas, she's helping her baby get up," Joseph observed, extending a lean, muscular arm from where he hung halfway over the rail. The oldest boy on the ranch at eighteen, Joseph was long, lanky and a good-natured encourager of the younger boys. He had his heart set on being a large-animal vet and Morgan knew he would make a great one someday.

"It's 'cause she *loves* her," ten-year-old Sammy whispered reverently, a whole host of wistfulness in his words that cut into Morgan's heart. Sammy had been at the ranch for only two weeks and was struggling. The kid's parents had given him up recently and before he could blink twice he found himself at Sunrise Ranch. The foster care worker had known the ranch had one opening and wasted no time getting Randolph and Morgan to accept Sammy into the mix. But Morgan could tell the poor kid was still grieving and in denial about what had happened to him.

Pepper's compassionate old eyes met Morgan's. These boys knew what it was to have a mother and a father who didn't care. Over the years Morgan had had many boys come to talk to him about how seeing a horse taking such tender care of her baby stabbed at their hearts on a raw level.

The first group of boys came to live at the ranch when Morgan was thirteen. They'd lost their parents, and because Morgan had just lost his mom to cancer two years earlier, he thought he understood what they were going through. It wasn't until he was a high school senior that he finally realized he didn't know where these boys were coming from at all. His mother had loved him with all of her heart. Death had forced her to leave her children—she never would have neglected or abandoned them.

It wasn't until six years ago when his fiancée gave back her engagement ring and chose a life without him that he felt some semblance of what these guys felt. It was a hard lick to know you weren't wanted.

For a moment, he went back to that day, standing in the drive, his heart in the dirt at his feet, watching Jolie Sheridan drive off into the wide blue yonder. He was over it—had been for some time now—but it had been a long, hard crawl out of the pit he'd fallen into. He'd made some mistakes on the way and fueled plenty of gossip in Dew Drop. But he'd lived.

He'd moved on.

He'd always known his life and dreams were here on the ranch, and even though things hadn't turned out exactly like he'd envisioned them, he'd managed to take hold of what God had entrusted to him and he was content.

Even happy most of the time.

At last the filly got her legs beneath her and managed to take her first wobbly steps, bringing Morgan back to the stable.

"She did it!" Jeb yelled. His nine-year-old enthusiasm startled the filly—she jumped and fell flat on her face.

Horrified, Jeb clamped his hand to the top of his head as the boys around him scowled. In the sudden silence the filly gathered herself up and this time rose more easily, with just a single nudge from her momma. Jeb gave a big silent grin. The excitement the boys were containing over the filly's accomplishment could very easily have blown the roof off the building.

There was a lot to be learned from what they'd just witnessed. Getting up from a fall was a life lesson well worth paying attention to.

"Okay, boys," Pepper said, coming out of the stall, "let's give mother and baby some alone time. You fellas can come back this evening after you get your chores done. You just have to promise to be quiet."

"Will do," agreed Wes, a stocky seventeen-year-old with curly blond hair and a cocky attitude. The boys looked up to Wes and Joseph, and the two teens took their leadership roles seriously. Morgan liked that about them.

By the time they were leaving the stable, rowdy laughter and joking had ensued. Morgan followed the group, somewhat calmer than he'd been on entering but still not pleased. His dad had deliberately made the decision about Jolie without him because he knew there was no way Morgan would have agreed to it. But Morgan's anger wasn't just based on personal grounds—in his estimation the last thing the fellas needed was another teacher who wouldn't stick around. And Jolie was *exactly* that.

As fate would have it, Morgan and the boys walked into the sunlight as Jolie herself whipped her cranberry-colored Jeep into the ranch yard, sliding to a halt across the driveway from them in a plume of dust. The doors and top were off the Jeep, giving them a clear view of her, with wind-tossed cinnamon hair.

Morgan's gut twisted in a knot and he came up short as if he'd slammed face-first into a flag pole. He had a clear shot of her. Rocks lodged in his throat. She was beautiful.

She had the boys' attention instantly, looking vibrant and full of life, every inch the world-class competitive kayaker that she was, long legs and tanned skin in well-worn jeans and a sleeveless orange tank top. She jumped from the vehicle with a big Julia Roberts smile on her face—and a hundred watts of pure joy slammed into the group.

It felt more like a sucker punch to Morgan.

"*Who* is *that?*" Joseph whistled as long strides brought her closer. There was no mistaking his admiration of Jolie. The kid was seventeen after all.

Wes elbowed Joseph out of the way. "Hubba, hubba, come to papa," he said. Morgan bopped him on the back of the head.

"Watch your manners, hotshot," he warned. "Both of you," he added as Joseph glanced at him, too.

"I didn't mean any harm," Wes said, his blue eyes dreamy. "I'm just in *lovvve*."

Joseph put his hand on his heart and patted it, then gave his full attention back to Jolie.

"She sure is pretty," Caleb gushed as she came nearer.

True on all counts—Morgan could not deny it. Jolie still had the ability to take his breath away.

"What's up, fellas? How's it going?" She greeted the guys like she'd just seen them yesterday and knew them by name. Looking like a bright beam of sunlight, she seemed to sparkle. She hadn't looked at Morgan yet, focusing all her attention on the sixteen totally engrossed fellas whose lower lips were now sitting firmly on their boot tips.

"You fellas must be my new class. I'm Jolie Sheridan, your teacher."

"You *are?*" Sammy cooed. The rest of them had suddenly become speechless.

"You bet I am." Jolie chuckled. "I'm excited to start school." Those luminescent green eyes met Morgan's for the first time and he was fairly certain he looked as grim as he felt because her smile faltered.

"We don't have to start today, do we?" Sammy blurted. Jolie gave them another sucker-punch grin as she put her focus back on the boys.

"Don't worry, little dude, school's not till Monday. You have freedom today and tomorrow…and then you're *all mine, all mine,*" she sang the last words and ended with a wink. "I'm just getting the classroom fixed up today."

The woman had skills when it came to winning over a crowd. Of course she'd had this fickle group at her first hello.

"I'd be glad to help you," Joseph offered, finally finding his voice.

Wes Grinned. "Count me in." His chest was so puffed out Morgan feared the teen would throw his back out of whack.

Their eagerness had Morgan rethinking some things…like maybe it was time to offer Joseph and Wes some guidance on relationships, and what was acceptable around a girl. Not that the boys were around girls very much because they went to school on the ranch. Still, there were local girls at church and around town. Morgan made a mental note.

Jolie's eyes widened at their offer. "I would *love* some help if you fellas want to. Only if Morgan doesn't have plans for you, though."

Every eye turned toward him.

"You don't, do you?" Joseph vocalized their question.

He wanted to say that yes, in fact, he sure did. He wanted nothing more than to tell the kids they had other things that required their attention besides Miss Jolie Sheridan. But any cowboy worth his salt knew when he was caught.

The right thing to do—the *courteous* thing to do—was help out the new teacher and offer assistance.

Him included.

If it had been any other person, he wouldn't have even hesitated.

"Nope," he heard himself saying. "No plans that can't wait. Helping Miss Sheridan get settled would be the gentlemanly thing to do, so we'll do that first and then we'll go build the fence."

"I don't want to disrupt any plans you've already made," she insisted.

The guys erupted like squawking geese, assuring her it was *no* problem. No problem at all.

Morgan suddenly wanted to take the boys and get as far away from Jolie as possible. But instead, he said, "Like the guys are telling you, it's not a problem. We can build the fence Monday after school if we don't get it done this afternoon."

She smiled at him and it hit him in the gut like a two-by-four. He was in for a beating while she was around, whether he wanted to admit it or not.

"Well, okay. Thanks."

"You're welcome," he said, his breath jamming in his throat.

She hesitated, her eyes locking on his for a second before turning back to the boys. Only then could Morgan breathe.

"If that's the case then follow me, good men that you are," she directed with a laugh. "Let's go see what adventures await us."

Waving to the fellas to follow her, she headed for

the three-room schoolhouse. The boys trotted behind her looking like a litter of puppies with their tongues hanging out.

Morgan watched them go. "Just call me Jolie," he heard her telling them, her voice drifting to him over the distance, like a long-forgotten song.

"I heard she was back." Pepper came out of the stable to stand beside him. "Your grandmother told me she stopped by the kitchen yesterday and said hello. She said they had a real nice visit. Said she was worried about you, though. Me, too. I figure from that scowl on your face you just found out this morning."

So even his grandmother knew.

"How many others knew about this?" he asked, not even trying to hide his anger.

"Don't get me to lying. I just happened to see her coming out of your dad's office yesterday when you and the boys were off working cattle with Rowdy. I asked your grandmother about it."

Morgan shook his head, watching Jolie in the distance. His stomach rolled like he'd just been thrown from a rough bronc. What had he been thinking when he'd offered to help?

Staring from beneath bushy eyebrows with concern, Pepper clapped Morgan on the back. "You hold your ground, Morg. Dig your boots into that gravel and don't budge. I helped scrape your heart up off the sidewalk once, and I ain't lookin' forward to doing it again in this lifetime."

Morgan shot him a firm look. "You don't have to worry about me. I learned my lesson a long time ago. I'm just looking out for the boys today."

"Good. I haven't ever disagreed with your dad about much, but this time I have to admit that I did. He should have never let that girl come back. It just ain't right, accident or no accident."

Morgan knew about the accident. His grandmother had told him how Jolie had nearly drowned in competition on a river. It hit him hard then and still did now, even if he had gotten over his feelings for her the day she'd given him back his ring.

Tugging his hat down low, he gave Pepper a nod and headed off toward the school. Might as well get this over with.

Despite the anger that still lived inside him, his pulse picked up speed as he started after Jolie. And his boots followed suit, not dragging anywhere near as much as he thought they should, considering he was going to help the woman who'd left him high and dry with his heart—and his engagement ring—in his hand.

Chapter Two

Did I make the right choice coming home to the ranch?

Jolie's emotions had been tumbling around inside her like clothes in a dryer since the moment she'd spotted Morgan standing beside the stables. The cowboy had always turned her world upside down with his midnight-black hair and deep blue eyes. Six feet of lean Texas cowboy with an extra inch added on for good measure—like the guy needed any extra help.

He'd been thirteen when she moved to the ranch with her parents. Immediately she'd thought he hung the moon. He'd probably thought she was a ten-year-old pest but was too kind to let her know it, unlike his brother Rowdy. Instead he'd endured her childish adoration with a patience that she'd tested on a regular basis.

How could she not have fallen in love with the guy?

"Where should this go?" Joseph asked, looking at her desk.

"I think I'd like it over there by that wall." Jolie pointed to the opposite side of the room from where the heavy oak desk was sitting now. She smiled, determined not to let the rush of the past and the uncertainty of the present distract her from getting her classroom set up.

She was impressed with the way the boys were willing to help. And startled and a bit shaken by the fact that Morgan had offered his help, too. Especially because he'd not hidden the fact that he was unhappy about her being here—his eyes had told the tale. She'd hoped time had healed old wounds, but even if it hadn't, she'd had to come home to the ranch.

Needed to come home.

Needed desperately to find the person she'd been, the person she'd lost somewhere in the depths of West Virginia's Gauley River.

She had loved Sunrise Ranch from the moment she'd moved here when her folks had been hired as house parents for one of the two foster homes on the ranch. It had been a wonderful place to grow up. And she was praying it would now be a place where she could heal and find the funny, take-the-world-by-the-horns girl she'd lost beneath the dark water of the Gauley.

The girl she was faking right now for these boys.

Coming up out of that water, her world shaken to its very core, the one thing she'd known upon gasping that first lifesaving breath was it was time to face her past....

Time to apologize to Morgan McDermott.

As if God was in agreement, this opportunity dropped in her lap and here she was.

"Is this where you want it...Jolie?" Joseph asked.

She'd told them right off to call her Jolie. She was just too laid back for anything else, even if she was their teacher. Besides, the ranch was home to the boys. Informality made it all the more true.

"Perfect," she said to the earnest young man.

"You got it, then." Joseph grabbed the edge of the monstrous desk and she was pretty sure he was about to try and move it himself. Not to be outdone, Wes was eyeing the floor-to-ceiling bookcases with determination.

"Hold off over there, Wes," Morgan demanded, coming in the front door and taking charge. Jolie's insides jangled as his presence filled the large room.

So much hung between them. She'd hoped to talk to him yesterday when she'd arrived, but he'd been working cattle at the far edge of the ranch. And so here they were in a room full of bright-eyed students, unable to talk about the fact that today had been their first meeting since she'd given him back his engagement ring.

"We'll get the desk moved first and then the bookshelves, Wes," Morgan said as he grabbed the other side of her desk.

"Thanks." Joseph grinned at Morgan. "We're putting it over there." He nodded his brown head toward the windows.

With Morgan's strength, the two were able to move the mammoth desk with ease. Once that was done they attacked the ten-foot-tall bookshelves. It ended up taking Morgan and most of the boys to move them.

Everyone's eagerness touched Jolie's heart.

She was smiling so much that she was almost able to ignore the fact that being around Morgan was causing her some heavy-duty stress—she could suddenly feel his presence like a weight.

"Where's our desks gonna sit, Jolie?"

Jolie looked down into the big, brown eyes of a wisp of a boy. "Sammy, right?" she asked, and he nodded. Sammy seemed like a nervous little fella. Uncertain of himself.

"We'll need to turn them all to face my desk. That way the light from the windows will stream across your desks. I *love* light and want y'all to enjoy it while you work."

"Can my desk be this one?" His words were as timid as the light touch he laid on the desk closest to hers, almost as if he were certain she would say no.

"Sure. It's got Sammy written all over it. Matter of fact, everyone can pick their desk."

Unsmiling, Sammy nodded and slipped into the wooden seat. "Only till my dad comes and gets me," he added in a quiet voice barely audible over the noise of the chaos breaking out behind him as the other boys began slamming into desks two at a time.

Jolie hardly even glanced at what was happening around her as her heart latched on to Sammy, who was so clearly suffering. "Sure," she assured him. "You can have that desk as long as you're here."

She wasn't sure what else to say. There were times when kids were on the ranch short-term. But most boys were here for the long haul—Sunrise Ranch had always been geared toward boys who had been totally abandoned by their families. The ranch became their home; the people, their family.

The poor kid got a wistful look on his face, then patted the desk next to him. "You can have this desk, Joseph," he called to Joseph—obviously Sammy's hero—as Joseph watched the rodeo going on over who got which desk.

"I'm too big to sit on the front row." Joseph brushed his brown bangs out of his eyes. "One of the shorter kids can sit there, and I'll sit in the back so I can make sure all you goofballs behave. Hey, goofballs!" he yelled, drawing all eyes in his direction. "One of you to a desk."

"Yeah," Wes barked loudly, crossing his arms and

stepping up beside Joseph. "What kind of *animals* are y'all anyway?"

It looked as if Wes and Joseph had decided they were going to make certain the boys behaved for her. Jolie hid a grin—and then her gaze met Morgan's. Morgan's eyebrow hitched upward, his dark denim eyes cool.

He has no confidence in me, she suddenly thought. Jolie was fairly certain Morgan would think she needed help in that department—if, that is, he even remembered how she'd let her class get out of control on her first day of student teaching. It had been a long time ago, and he might have easily forgotten the laugh they'd shared over the little boys letting the mice out of their cage and the hysterics that had ensued. Meeting his sardonic gaze, she hiked a brow of her own. "It'll be okay, guys. They're just excited. We're going to be fine," she said to Wes and Joseph, assuring all of them, as well as herself.

"Can you ride a horse?" Sammy asked, drawing her attention. She was grateful for the change of subject.

"Yes, I can. Can you?" she asked.

He shook his head. "Never been on one."

"He helped us work cattle yesterday, though." Morgan stepped up beside the boy, giving him a smile that sent an arrow straight to Jolie's heart. Morgan McDermott had a soft spot for these boys.

He placed a hand on Sammy's shoulder. "You did good, Sammy."

"It was scary. I almost got trampled, too." Sammy's eyes were huge.

"Aw, come on, kid, it wasn't that bad," Joseph called from the back of the room where he was trying out his new desk. "If you stick with us, you'll learn not to be scared."

Sammy didn't look too sure about that.

"I ride," yelped Tony, a skinny kid around fifteen or so who looked like a young Elvis Presley with his swath of black hair, blue eyes and a crooked smile that made his eyes twinkle. He skidded to a halt in front of Jolie.

This led each boy to reveal he could ride. Jolie caught the flicker of fear in Sammy's expression as he realized he was the only one who couldn't ride. She glanced at Morgan to find his guarded eyes staring back at her.

"We're gonna learn to mug steers tomorrow after church," Caleb said, his freckles crinkling with his smile. "You can come, too, Jolie."

Sammy slipped his hand into hers and looked up. "Would you come?"

Jolie melted right there in the middle of the room. Turned right into a pool of liquid. "Sure I will," she said. She was pretty sure she would have jumped from an airplane if he'd asked her. "I love to calf wrestle, and scramble, too. But muggin' is my favorite! I used to be one of the best here on the ranch, you know."

"Seriously?" Joseph jerked to his feet, gaping at her from across the room. He and Wes exchanged disbelieving looks. "*You* can take down a steer?"

Jolie nearly shook her head. *Males.*

"Hey, y'all look like you don't think I can do it!" she teased.

"We just aren't used to girls—I mean, *women*—wantin' to do something like that," Wes drawled, glancing at Joseph and Tony.

Jolie smiled at the cocky, young cowboys, with their worn jeans tucked into their rugged boots and their T-shirts with the arms cut out of them. It was obvious that they'd been working that morning, most likely hauling hay, an ongoing job she remembered quite well growing up on the ranch. A picture of Morgan in that same getup at that age raced through her head and she glanced his way. He looked about as happy as a grizzly bear that had been awakened in the middle of a really good nap.

"I'm a little insulted here! Girls do this sort of thing all the time." She laughed when they all swallowed and looked a bit meek. "You'll find for the most part that I look at life with a bring-it-on attitude." She looked directly at Morgan before shifting back to the boys. "I haven't done it in a long time, but it sounds too fun to pass up. I'll be there." She looked at Mr. Grizzly Bear again. "May I speak to you outside?"

"Sure," he growled, swiveling toward the back door. "You boys don't tear anything up while we're gone."

Jolie thought Morgan was teasing even though he seemed far from a teasing mood. Surely he wasn't thinking the boys were going to destroy all the work they'd just put in. But then again, there *was* the incident with the desks.

Looking back over her shoulder, she was struck by the group. The picture they made reminded her of an old John Wayne movie, *The Cowboys,* about a bunch of ragtag boys who'd needed a gruff old cowboy to teach them life lessons. Although Morgan was far from an old cowboy, it was plain to see that these boys respected and admired him. And needed him.

Smiling at them, she winked. "If y'all want to finish turning the desks and lining them up, that would be great."

They all chorused, "Yes, ma'am."

Smiling at their politeness, she followed Mr. Grizzly outside and then passed him, leading him out of earshot of the class. There was a large, gnarled oak tree still bent over as it had been all those years ago. She didn't stop until she reached it, turning his way only after they were beneath the wide expanse of limbs.

Morgan crossed his arms and studied the tree. "I remember having to climb up this tree and talk you down after you scrambled up to the top and froze."

She hadn't expected him to bring up old memories—it caught her off guard. "I remember how mad you were at having to rescue the silly little new girl." Mad? Actually, furious was more accurate.

A hint of a smile teased his lips, fraying Jolie's nerves at the edges. It had been a long, long time since she'd seen that smile.

"I got used to it, though," he said, his voice warming.

She laughed, encouraged by his teasing. "You had no other choice! I guess if you hadn't rescued me I'd never have made it to my teen years." But she was grateful to Morgan for more than that. She'd grown into a teenager who could handle almost any situation, a girl confident in her own skin. She hadn't been afraid to try anything because she'd been so crazy adventurous—and free to learn from her mistakes, thanks to Morgan and his brothers, Rowdy and Tucker, who had always been there to help her through. She'd idolized them, but at the same time, wanted them to stop babying her.

Morgan especially.

Of course it was Morgan who'd made her the angriest, and Morgan whom she'd fallen for. Their relationship had never been an easy one. The push and pull of attraction had started when she'd demanded independence, and then changed when she'd found herself desperate for his approval. But it became something incredibly complicated when she'd realized she wanted his love.

And then the pull of competitive kayaking entered the equation when Morgan introduced her to it on a lazy summer afternoon and things grew more complicated. She'd been fifteen, and her instant infatuation with the sport had been too much to ignore. For a young woman who craved the adventure world-class competition offered, Sunrise Ranch suddenly seemed…small. When Morgan made it clear that he had no desire to leave the ranch, Jolie decided she had no choice but to walk away.

Looking at him now, she was overcome by the memory of the internal war she'd lived through when she'd made the decision to leave.

It had been six years, but it felt like twenty.

They were standing beneath the shade of the old oak tree, electricity humming between them. When the smile left Morgan's eyes, Jolie sucked in a wobbly breath, forcing herself to focus on the job she'd been hired to do. "I'm curious about Sammy. Has he been here long?"

"Just a couple of weeks. He's our newest rancher. He's still having trouble emotionally, after his abandonment. It's a tough situation."

"He seems fearful."

"He is, poor kid. He knows his dad has been gone from the picture for a long time. But his mother gave him up to the state and now he thinks his dad will find out and come for him. He'll stretch the truth from here to Alaska, so you might want to tread lightly with everything he says until you give it a reality check."

"He lies?" she asked, a little more frankly than she'd intended. But she needed to know the truth if she was going to help him.

Morgan grimaced. "Kinda. More like the boy who cried wolf."

"The stories don't ever seem to change, do they, Morgan? I just can't imagine how these boys handle their families not wanting them. Or not caring enough to make loving homes for them."

She'd been around kids like Sammy all the time growing up. Some handled the situation with anger, some with denial, but it was all about fear. She understood that on a personal level—three times this week she'd awakened in the middle of the night because of nightmares. She pushed the thoughts away, praying she was up for this job.

"Sammy's a good example of how bad these kids have been hurt. They need people around them who will care for them and stick with them." The hardness of Morgan's tone matched the accusation in his eyes. "What are you doing here, Jolie? Why aren't you taming rapids in some far-off place?"

"I...I'm—" She stumbled over her words, tongue-tied by his question. "I'm taking a leave from competition for a little while. I had a bad run in Virginia and I— It was bad." She couldn't bring herself to say that she'd almost died, that she was lucky to be standing there. "Anyway, your dad was kind enough to offer me this opportunity."

"I heard about the accident and I'm real sorry about that, Jolie. I really am. I wish you a speedy recovery so you can get back out there doing what you love. But why come here after all this time? We dropped off your radar a long time ago."

"This is my *home*. It has never been off my radar." Jolie saw anger in Morgan's eyes. Well, he had a right to it, and more than a right to point it straight at her. She'd just thought she was prepared for it.

She was wrong.

"Morgan," Jolie said, almost as a whisper. "I'd hoped we could forget the past and move forward."

Heart pounding, she reached across the space between them and placed her hand on his arm. It was just a touch, but the feeling of connecting with Morgan McDermott again after so much time rocked her straight to the core and suddenly she wasn't so sure coming home had been the right thing to do, after all.

A jolt from a live wire couldn't have burned Morgan more than the touch of Jolie's hand. Shock waves coursed through him with a vengeance, his mouth went dry. There had been a time when he'd have done anything for her touch. He gulped hard and hardened his heart against a walk down memory lane.

He wasn't some kid anymore, holding his heart in his hands. He was a thirty-two-year-old adult male with a good brain between his ears. Or at least he'd thought he had a good brain.

"I did forget the past. A long time ago," he assured her, his skin burning where her hand still lay. He wondered if she felt the way his pulse had started galloping at her touch. They stared at each other as seconds slipped by.

"Yes, of course you would have," Jolie said at last, her hand squeezing his arm slightly before it slipped away. "But I was hoping there would be no hard feelings."

His jaw jerked in reflex.

"I didn't mean to hurt you," she said. "It really wasn't personal."

"You broke our engagement, then headed off in search of *better* things. I think I had a right to take that personal."

"That is not fair."

Morgan was suddenly not at all comfortable with where this was heading.

"I wasn't searching for *better,*" she said. "I couldn't

stay. You know I would have regretted it for the rest of my life."

"Well," he drawled icily, "that makes me feel a whole heap better."

"I'm sorry," she said, her eyes shadowing. "Morgan, I'm so sorry for the way it ended that day. I'm sorry for letting us go so far. I never meant to hurt you. I never should have accepted the ring in the first place knowing my heart was torn."

"On that we agree." At least she hadn't waited until the night before they were to walk down the aisle like Celia, the next woman he'd been fool enough to ask to marry him. Two in a row had made Morgan hang up any thoughts of ever popping the question again. Not that he ever should have started dating Celia in the first place.

"Look, Jolie, that was a long time ago. It doesn't matter anymore. Right now my concern is for those boys. They got hung out to dry by their parents and then their teacher left them for something better at the last minute. They don't need another person leaving. They need someone they can count on to be here for them."

Slapping a hand on her hip, fire flashed in her eyes. "I intend to honor my contract for the semester, and I'm going to do my best to help each of the boys any way that I can."

Morgan met her gaze with fire of his own. "I don't like your being here, but it doesn't matter—you are. I'll just have to hope and pray it all turns out okay."

Turning away he strode back toward the schoolhouse, leaving Jolie standing beneath the old oak. He used the walk to rein in his temper so he could finish setting up the classroom. The last thing he needed was for the boys to pick up on the bad vibes between him and Jolie—and if he wasn't careful, they would, before he even made it in the door.

How, he wanted to know as the schoolhouse got closer and his temper just got worse, was he ever going to make this work?

Infuriating man, Jolie thought, stalking after Morgan. "Stop right where you are, bucko," she demanded, sounding as if she was calling him out to a gunfight at the O.K. Corral. He swung around at the entrance to the schoolhouse, clearly startled. She marched straight up to him.

"You might not have any faith in me." *And my faith in myself might be shaken to the core.* "But while I'm here, I'll give these kids everything I have to give. No holding back."

For the first time since the accident Jolie felt a familiar strength ease through her, and she liked it. She'd had moments since nearly drowning when she'd felt as weak as a newborn, but she still counted herself a strong woman. She prayed that throwing herself into helping the boys of Sunrise Ranch would be a win-win situation for all of them.

"Key words, Jolie—*while you are here.*"

"It doesn't matter to you if I can do a good job, does it, Morgan? This is personal on your part."

"You bet it's personal. These boys are my *personal* responsibility."

Stung by his words and breathless with fury, she glared up at him, trying to ignore the fact that the man smelled of pine and leather. His scent played havoc with her senses. Her eyes, traitors that they were, slid down to rest on his lips. She inhaled, but all the air in the world seemed to have gone missing.

Focus, Jolie. Focus.

"Think the worst of me, Morgan McDermott. However," she said, her conviction ringing true in her own ears, "I will give these boys everything I have to give them."

He stepped so close they were almost touching, and she had to tilt her head back to look him in the eye. "That's exactly what I expect," he said. "They deserve it." His gaze fell to her lips and lingered for only a brief instant before meeting hers. Jolie's heart skipped a beat, and Morgan's eyes were nearly black with dark emotion—yearning? Fury? Jolie was rendered speechless by his scowl. What was going on in that mind of his?

He left her then, continuing toward the school.

As she followed him toward the back door, she was sure of one thing and one thing only: for the first time in weeks she was filled with a great sense of purpose. What God had in store for her and Morgan, she didn't have a clue. But God had plans for her at the Sunrise Ranch school and she was determined to prove herself to Him.

It was probably going to be a lot easier than proving herself to Morgan.

Chapter Three

When Jolie reached the main classroom a few seconds after Morgan, she saw Joseph holding the front door open for Morgan's grandmother, Ruby Ann "Nana" McDermott. Nana was the backbone of the ranch, a former barrel racer who ran the chow hall like a well-greased wagon wheel. Her vision had been essential in making Lydia McDermott's dream come true, and her heart had been essential in making the place what it was today.

Jolie knew that since Lydia's death, Nana had been just as much a mother to Morgan as she had been to the countless young ranchers who'd needed her love. Jolie had loved and adored Nana and the feeling had been mutual. In her sixties, Nana had deep blue, wide-set eyes, high cheekbones and a square jaw, and there was no denying that her son Randolph and her three grandsons, Morgan, Rowdy and Tucker, were from her gene pool. Before her thick ponytail had turned the color of pale steel, it had been jet-black like Morgan's and Randolph's—a long-ago gift of the Cherokee blood of Nana's ancestors.

Yesterday Jolie had been welcomed by Nana with open arms—there was never any lack of hugs where

Nana was concerned. Today Nana hustled into the room like a woman on a mission, her ponytail swinging as she brought cookies to her boys—and checked up on Morgan and "her girl," as she always called Jolie.

She set the large tray down on a worktable beside the computer as the tantalizing scent of chocolate and cinnamon filled the room. Nana's smile was just as warm and sweet as the cookies nestled on the tray.

"Y'all have sure been workin' hard today, so I whipped up some of your favorite cookies." The instant she stepped back, it was like a free-for-all—the boys dived for the chocolate chip cookies, attacking them as if they hadn't eaten all morning.

"Glad you came on out today, Jolie," she said as Jolie gave her a hug.

"I thought it would be best to come and, you know—" she faltered as she looked at Morgan, who frowned at her "—get acquainted, with the boys, I mean, and get prepared."

Morgan looked as if he'd just witnessed her robbing a bank or something, his eyes narrowing in distrust. Jolie gulped and looked back at Nana.

"Thank you for the snacks. These boys deserve it—as you said, they've been working hard."

Nana waved off the comment. "These bottomless pits always need cookies." She planted her fists on her hips, giving Jolie and Morgan the once-over. "When I was coming out of the chow hall I saw you two heading around the back of the building."

Nana looked at Morgan, and Jolie thought she saw worry in her eyes.

"Um, we had things to discuss," Jolie explained. What else could she say?

"Morgan, how's your day going?" Nana asked when

it was obvious the boys were too engrossed in cookie devouring to eavesdrop on their conversation.

Exasperation flashed in Morgan's eyes. "How do you think, Nana? Started out with a real bang in Dad's office this morning."

Nana blushed—surprising Jolie, since she wasn't the blushing kind—and she leaned in close to Morgan. "If it makes you feel any better, I told Randolph he needed to warn you."

"And what about you?" he asked.

"I— Well," she said, patting his arm. "We'll talk about this later."

Jolie wasn't sure what was going on, but it sounded as if Morgan hadn't known she was coming. Was that possible? The thought practically made her gasp. If that was the case, then no wonder he was so hostile. His dad had not only made the decision to hire her on his own, but had also kept it a secret—until today.

"You didn't know?" she whispered.

His lips pressed into a tight line and his left eyebrow lifted ever so slightly.

Jolie gasped, looking from Morgan to Nana. It was true—Randolph hadn't told him!

Nana turned to where the boys were scarfing down the cookies as if there was no tomorrow. "Did you fellas know Jolie is a world-class champion kayaker? She gets paid by sponsors to travel all over the world and compete using their gear. Isn't that right, Jolie?"

"Get outta here. For real?" Wes said, stepping away from the cookie fray.

Jolie nodded and her stomach dropped to her feet as a sick feeling washed over her in a wave. *Please don't go there. I can't handle that right now on top of everything else.*

She'd known it was ridiculous to hope no one would mention her kayaking, yet she'd hoped exactly that. She gave a weak smile. "I've won a few competitions."

"Ha!" Nana hooted. "She's top ten in the country."

Morgan crossed his arms, his expression stormy.

"Top in the country!" Wes gushed, suddenly looking a lot younger than seventeen.

"Really?" Tony joined in, his eyes lit with expectations.

Alarms clanged inside of Jolie.

"What's kayaking?" Caleb asked as he and the other smaller fellas looked up from their cookies.

"It's like a plastic canoe that holds one person, and they compete on riding the rapids and stuff." Joseph had come closer, as intent as Wes and Tony. "We have some rapids on the river at this place. Do you know that?"

She knew what was coming next. She knew it and she wasn't even sure she could speak. But she nodded and fought for words as acid churned in her stomach.

"I—I started on those rapids when I was a kid. Morgan showed them to me."

That was all the encouragement the boys needed. They instantly erupted in excitement.

"Cool! Can you teach us?" Joseph said over the others' exclamations. Jolie silently prayed for God to help her.

"I've always wanted to learn," Wes gushed again, grinning like he'd just won the lottery. "Can you teach us?" he echoed as the others chimed in.

Jolie's vision blurred—where had all the air gone? She suddenly felt unbearably hot as every eye in the room stared at her. Her pulse pounded in her head like the roar of the white river rapids she now feared. Black spots began to spatter her vision like paint drops. She swayed, woozy, and her gaze swung to Morgan—for what? To ask for help?

I can't teach these boys to kayak!

Breathe, she commanded herself, even as her knees turned to jelly….

"Jolie!"

Morgan's voice rumbled down a long tunnel as Jolie sank like a rock.

One minute she was standing and the next she was swooped up into strong arms. *His* strong arms. Morgan McDermott's arms.

The arms she'd longed for since she'd walked away from Sunrise Ranch…six long years ago….

Voices floated to Jolie through a dark fog.

"She fainted," Caleb gasped.

"Passed smooth out," Sammy said in a hushed voice.

"I ain't never in my whole long life seen nobody pass out," B.J. whispered.

Though lost in the fog, it registered loud and clear to Jolie that her head was resting against Morgan's chest. His heart beat against her temple so hard it was no wonder she'd come to so quickly.

"Good thang you gone and caught her, Morgan," B.J. continued. Jolie was surprised how easily she could already identify the boys just by the sound of their voices.

"Yeah, or she might have died," Sammy said solemnly.

"Caleb and Sammy, how about y'all get me a glass of water and a cold rag?" Nana urged gently.

"Sure! I'll get the rag," Caleb volunteered.

"I'll get the water," Sammy said. Their voices were followed immediately by the trample of feet.

"Jolie, can you hear me?" Morgan asked gently.

Jolie lifted her eyes and forced herself to pull her head

away from Morgan's heart. Embarrassment warmed her face. "Faint of heart" was not a description of the gal who'd looked down the throat of The Gorilla—the burliest rapids in the toughest of all the extreme kayaking competitions in the world—and felt only an adrenaline rush and excitement. She was not a wimp. Fainting was *not* in her vocabulary…or at least it hadn't been until she'd almost drowned.

"Give her some air, boys," Nana said. Moving in, she fanned Jolie furiously with a booklet she must have snatched from the bookshelf. "Honey, you're whiter than Walter Pepper's hair!"

Jolie would have smiled at that if she could have.

"How are you doing?" Morgan asked, his voice gruff in a way that made her heart beat faster.

"I'm okay," Jolie assured them, looking at Morgan. His eyes were full of concern—and questions. She was thankful they were surrounded by the boys—boys who were silent and looked a little scared. She needed to stand up and show them she was fine.

Even if she was fast becoming a wimp, she certainly didn't have to broadcast it.

"Are you sure?" Morgan set her on her feet, keeping his arms around her. "Maybe you should sit down."

Maybe I need to stay in your arms—

Maybe I need to get a grip!

"No, I can stand," she said firmly, and forced herself to step away from Morgan.

The concern in his eyes almost undid her.

This was the man she'd fallen for when she was sixteen years old. This was a gentler man, not the hard man she'd been dealing with for the last couple of hours. Sadly, she knew she was partly to blame for some of the hard crust encasing Morgan.

Praying her witless knees wouldn't buckle, she was pleased when she stood firm. All she had to do now was come up with an answer as to why she wasn't going to teach the boys how to kayak.

Sammy and Caleb came bounding from the back of the building, Caleb waving a washcloth and Sammy sloshing water from the glass as he ran, the hand clamped tightly over the glass not keeping the water from escaping. His big eyes were huge with fear. She hated that she'd worried him when he already had so many things bothering him.

"Sit," Morgan demanded, pushing her into the nearest seat. B.J. immediately came to stand beside her.

"You're whiter than a marshmallow," Caleb declared, pushing the washcloth into her hands.

"I'm fine," she assured him and the others as they all began talking about how pale she was.

"You scared fifteen years off my life," Sammy said, sounding like an adult.

Jolie had to chuckle at his tone.

"Sammy, you don't have fifteen years to scare off," Joseph teased. "You're only ten."

Sammy frowned. "She scared it off me, though."

Caleb blinked hard. "You scared me, too."

Jolie's heart warmed at their worry. "I'll be honest with you, fellas. It freaked me out a little, too. I mean, really, I blacked out and woke up in Mr. Morgan's arms—*that's* a scary thing!"

She won a round of laughter from all the boys, and keeping the momentum going, she drove the topic away from her. The last thing she wanted was for one of them to ask about kayaking again.

She caught Morgan watching her and her insides did a

swan dive straight to her toes. Forcing her chin upward, she gave him a smile and kept her balance as she stood.

Joseph frowned, his lean face looking a little strange without the smile that was usually plastered across it. "You're as wobbly as the filly we just saw born."

"I'm okay." She forced any shakiness from her voice. "Now, let's talk about this calf wrestling I'll be winning tomorrow."

"Winning?" Joseph grinned dubiously, looking more like himself. "I don't think so. I'm wrestling, too."

"Me, too," Wes spoke up, challenge in his eyes. "Which means y'all are lookin' at the winner right here." He pulled his thumbs toward his chest and grinned.

Jolie laughed, feeling some semblance of herself returning. "You boys need to remember to never underestimate your opponent." She let her gaze slide to Morgan. He crossed his arms and cocked his head to the side, his eyes holding steady, assessing her.

She knew she wasn't fooling him. She also knew it wouldn't be long before he asked her exactly what the fainting was all about.

She wondered if he would ask purely out of concern, as any decent person would do, or if he would ask because somewhere behind that shield he wore, he still cared for her. She was just going to have to wait and see.

But in the meantime, she should probably figure out what to do about the fact that she desperately wanted it to be the latter.

Chapter Four

A little unhinged by her afternoon, Jolie headed straight for the Spotted Cow Café to see her longtime friend Ms. Jo. The café was in its mid-afternoon lull when she walked through the lemon pie–yellow door. She was immediately greeted by the moo of the four-foot toy cow just inside the entrance. The cow's hide had bare spots on it from years of kids petting it, but it mooed like a newborn bawling after its mama.

Jolie had good memories in this diner.

The soft buttery walls were covered with all manner of spotted-cow gifts from customers: knickknacks, cattle horns and mooing cow clocks were everywhere. It was a unique place, to say the least. Even the buffed-concrete floor was painted with large, irregularly shaped brown spots. They were supposed to represent the hide of a spotted cow but had come out looking more like cow patties, which was why Chili Crump and Drewbaker Macintosh, a couple of the old-time locals, nicknamed the diner the Cow Patty Café. Needless to say, that made Ms. Jo furious.

Jolie headed for the old-fashioned soda fountain at the back and her mouth began to water the instant the glass case of frothy pies came into view. Her stomach growled, reminding her that she hadn't eaten all day.

Pie sounded like the perfect meal after the day she'd had.

"That'll make you fat," Edwina, the longtime waitress, warned, hustling out of the back carrying plates of hamburgers and fries. She paused to give Jolie a lopsided grin. "But it's worth every calorie and more. You can tell by my hips that I partake of a bite every chance I can get."

Jolie chuckled. Edwina was a character who'd worked for Ms. Jo for years. Skin as tough as boot leather and a personality to match, Edwina loved to tell tall tales. Rough as she was, she was part of the atmosphere and as dependable as all the cow clocks put together.

"You here to see Ms. Jo?" she asked. "She's armpit-high in pie crust—okay, so her armpits aren't involved, but she *is* in the pie dough, if you want to find her."

Jolie grinned. "Thanks, Ed. You keeping the cowboys straight today?"

Edwina huffed and headed toward the two cowboys sitting at the window. "Crazy men, I done told them they weren't welcomed in here but they keep comin'. I know it's not the food or my winning personality, so it's got to be my beauty. It's a curse."

Chuckling, Jolie headed through the swinging doors. She'd made Ms. Jo mad when she'd first arrived in town and only taken time to get checked in at the Dew Drop Inn before heading out to see Randolph. She'd known Harvey, the front-desk clerk, would have it all over town that she was back. By the time Jolie had come in yesterday afternoon, Ms. Jo had been told and was not happy that Jolie hadn't come by to see her. She was probably still a little peeved about it today.

Walking through the curtain into the large, spotless kitchen, Jolie waved at T-Bone, their cook, as she passed the grill and went back to the baking area. Ms. Jo, a compact little gal with short brown hair curled around her ears, worked the dough with a pie roller. Her alert hazel eyes locked onto Jolie as she entered the room.

"I know that look," she quipped, rolling pin wagging at Jolie. "You met up with Morgan, didn't you?"

Jolie gave a weary nod as it all settled down on her again. Keeping her energy up for the kids had been tough, and she was emotionally drained.

"By the looks of you, it didn't go so well." Pointing the rolling pin at the stool by the workstation, she demanded, "Sit down and talk to me." Heading to the sink, she rinsed her hands under the faucet. "How did Morgan react to seeing you?"

Jolie made circles in a small pile of white flour that was on the counter. "He isn't happy. At all."

"What did you expect? Flowers? You *did* hand him back his ring before hitting the trail for parts unknown."

"Gee, thanks for the support."

"You know I love you, but I'm worryin' you're fixin' to get yourself in some hot water."

"I apologized and he didn't take it well." She didn't go into the fainting episode. The last thing she wanted to talk about was the reaction she'd had to being in his arms.

Shrewd eyes held Jolie's. "You hurt Morgan when you left. And then, on the rebound, that boy went and almost married Celia Simpson. And she left him right after the rehearsal." Ms. Jo clucked her tongue. "I'd hate to see you lead Morgan down the wrong road again."

"I would never do that. Besides, he can barely stand to look at me."

"You know he's one of my favorites, Jolie. Kind of reminds me a little of my Clovis. He's got feelings that run real deep and it'll take more than words to prove you're sorry. But maybe working with those boys he loves so much will help."

Jolie was glad Ms. Jo didn't tell her it would be easy—they both knew it wouldn't be. Ms. Jo pulled a pie out of the glass icebox. "How about you and me take a break and have us a piece of this lemon pie with some coffee?"

Jolie sat up at attention. "Do you even have to ask?" She wondered if pie would help erase the feel of Morgan's arms around her. Her heart went erratic just thinking about how she'd felt snuggled against his heart....

"I think this situation is gonna need a bunch of prayers, too. For those boys' sakes, we need you two on speaking terms. Y'all don't have to make up and kiss or anything—goodness knows that would only lead things in the wrong direction. Just bury the hatchet and get it over with."

"Easier said than done, I think."

"In all honesty, this could be the best thing for Morgan." Ms. Jo brightened. "Maybe it'll help him move forward, find someone who'll actually go through with marrying him. Seems such a waste for a cowboy of his caliber not to have someone to call his own."

Jolie put a huge bite of lemon pie on her fork, breathed in the tangy scent and stuffed it in her mouth so she wouldn't have to say anything.

Because even after all this time, the thought of Morgan and someone else made Jolie want to eat an entire case of pies.

"How you doing, Morg, my man?" Rowdy asked Sunday afternoon.

Rowdy, Morgan's younger brother, ran the ranch's

cattle operation and they were sorting the steers for the mugging together. "My boots almost had blowouts when Dad told me what he'd done."

"You think *you* had a blowout," Morgan growled.

Rowdy, who always looked as if he was ready for a good time, with lips that turned up at the edges and eyes shot with mischief, looked as concerned as Morgan had ever seen him. "So how did it go? The boys about talked my ear off at lunch. They're impressed, just in case you didn't know that."

"Thanks, I picked up on that all by myself when their jaws started dragging in the dirt. And Wes and Joseph started showing off their muscles."

Rowdy's lips twitched. "Should make for a good show tonight. But how are you?"

Morgan rested a boot on the bottom rung of the arena and studied the steers closely. "How do you think? I don't have a choice but to deal with it."

"Maybe that's a good thing." Rowdy hiked a shoulder. "You don't date, Morg. You act like you're married to the school. You have unfinished business and it's time to finish it, one way or the other."

Morgan grunted and kept his mouth shut.

"Would you look at that?" Rowdy whistled over the bellowing of cattle. "Pest is lookin' good."

Morgan turned to see Jolie hopping from her Jeep.

"Yeah," he snapped. "Tell me something I don't already know."

Rowdy chuckled, crossed his arms and leaned back against the corral to watch Jolie. Morgan shot him a glare, not fond of that glint in his brother's eyes.

"I thought you said you were all right," Rowdy said.

"I'm not in the mood, Rowdy."

"Touché. Don't get me wrong, I'm on your side. You

got a real raw deal, but maybe that was all she had to give you at the time. Like I said, this could be a good thing."

"Maybe I don't want to discuss this right now."

Rowdy chuckled. "Like I said, *touché*. Got to go get myself a hug." Pushing off the fence, he strode toward Jolie, who had stopped to talk to their dad. Tucker, the eldest of the McDermott boys, was the county sheriff. He'd been talking with Nana, and now they all headed Jolie's way.

Morgan scrubbed his scratchy jaw—it had been a long night delivering a new foal, he hadn't had much sleep and this morning he'd missed church. He was *not* in the mood for this.

"Hey, pest," Rowdy drawled, using his pet name for Jolie. "You're looking good, but a little on the thin side. You not eating out there, making all that money having your picture taken in that yellow banana of yours?"

"Rowdy!" Jolie exclaimed. Rowdy laid an arm across her shoulders and hugged her as if she was his long-lost friend.

"Jolie." Tucker greeted her with a hug, too.

Morgan almost got lockjaw, grinding his molars watching, his dad grinning as though he'd just reunited the family.

Ten thousand acres of West Texas ranch lands suddenly didn't feel big enough. This "reunion" was enough to make a man ride off into the sunset and never look back.

"Hey, Morgan." Chet, one of the top hands, called from the cattle pens on the far side of the barn. "Got a sec?"

A couple of years younger than he was, Chet had grown up on the ranch as a foster kid and had stayed on. Like the other fifteen cowboys who worked for the ranch, he knew Morgan's history with Jolie…and Celia. There had been no teasing so far, and that fact alone told him they all thought he was on shaky ground now that Jolie was back.

It was embarrassing.

"I hear you fainted yesterday," his dad said as Morgan hit the fast track across the corral toward Chet.

He'd had Jolie's fainting spell on his mind since it had happened. Something was up with her, and he figured the last place she needed to be was running up and down this arena trying to throw a yearling on its back with her bare hands. Of course she lived in a world where she took her life in her hands every time she got into that kayak of hers and plowed through raging white water *and* over ridiculous waterfalls that weren't meant for humans to fall over, much less charge over on purpose.

And to think he'd been the one to introduce her to it. Little had he known she would fall for it and become one of the best. When he'd taken her kayaking as a kid, it had been slow, easy river runs, nothing life-threatening—

He stopped his thoughts in their tracks.

Jolie wasn't his concern anymore—hadn't been since the day she'd walked away, choosing kayaking over him.

"What's up?" he growled, reaching Chet.

Nudging his Stetson off his forehead, Chet met Morgan's look with frank brown eyes. "Thought the love and admiration was about to start piling up knee-deep to a giraffe over there," he drawled sarcastically, then pointed at one of the steers. "This 'un here's got a bad leg. Thought you'd want to pull it from the event."

That was no-nonsense Chet. Said what he wanted and moved on. Morgan almost grinned. Chet wasn't one to get in another person's business—giving him his support by saying what he just had meant a lot to Morgan.

Morgan studied the limping steer. “Yeah, take him out.”

“Will do, boss.” Chet nodded to one of the other cowboys working the gate to open it up. He and Morgan flanked the steer to send him through the gate, and one of the other cowboys herded him toward a separate pen.

“Time to get ready for some fun.”

Chet nodded. “Sounds good to me.”

Watching him head off to gather the men, Morgan knew Chet had his back. That was more than he could say about his own family. Although maybe his brothers’ affection for Jolie could come in handy. She might not want to tell him about the fainting episode, but that didn’t mean she wouldn’t tell Rowdy or Tucker. Regardless, Morgan was determined to find out what was going on, whether Jolie wanted him to or not.

Chapter Five

The familiar scent of dirt and cattle filled the air as Jolie tried hard *not* to watch Morgan. It was an almost-impossible feat—the man had gotten only better-looking in the past six years. His black hair curled out from under his hat, just whispering against his blue button-down. The color made his eyes look darker than ever. And he was in his element as he strode back and forth inside the arena with Rowdy and the other cowboys getting everything set up for the mugging.

"I got trampled by a cow one time. That's why I'm afraid to go out there," Sammy was saying to Jolie. He'd been shadowing her since she'd arrived at the arena. Something about the kid spoke to her, and she wondered why he'd gravitated toward her. She couldn't help thinking that it was the fear eating him up that had drawn him to her. Maybe on a subconscious level he recognized a kindred spirit of sorts.

Because she had fear eating her up, too.

And it irritated the dickens out of her. So much so that despite almost no sleep, she'd dragged herself out of bed and made it to church on just one cup of coffee. Her night had been awful, to say the least—just plain terrible.

It had started with thoughts of Morgan—specifically, the feel of his arms around her and the beat of his heart in her ear. Those sensations kept her awake half the night. When she'd finally fallen asleep, the nightmares arrived. Why, oh, why had she thought coming home would help ease them?

They hadn't eased one iota.

Instead, they'd come as hard as ever, if not more so. Always the same, she was trapped in a raging vortex, upside down and fighting to make it to the surface. Always ensnared and struggling for her life.

Somewhere in the wee hours of the morning she'd given up trying to sleep and lay covered in sweat, tangled in sheets and worn-out. In the month since the accident, this had become the norm. Usually she turned to her Bible, searching for comfort and peace. Even though peace had been elusive, she knew God and only God had brought her up out of that watery grave.

A person would think that if she knew *God* had yanked her out of that murky water, there would be no reason to be full of fear from her toes to her roots—but she was. And she didn't know what to do about it.

"You're scared?" According to Morgan, Sammy was prone to exaggerations so she wasn't sure what to make of his remark about being trampled, but she certainly recognized fear when she saw it. And it was like a flashing red beacon in his eyes.

He nodded. "Scared bad."

"That's totally understandable. Did the cow hurt you very badly?"

His gaze slid left, then back toward the four-foot-tall steers. "Broke my leg. My dad, he took real good care of me, though. And my mom." He paused, gulping. "She cried, it scared her so bad." He sighed wistfully. "They loved me so much they hated to see it happen."

Heart *slam!*—Jolie was suddenly desperately grateful for her parents' love and affection. She wanted to hug the child close—and at the same time do bodily harm to his parents for giving him up.

"I'm sure they did." Jolie wondered if he even realized he'd said "loved" in the past tense. "You remember that anytime you need to talk about them, or anything that scares you, you can come to me. If you want to," she added.

A half smile appeared that was one day going to make female hearts stop.

What a cute kid. And what a tough road he'd traveled. As had most of these boys.

A steer broke from the pack at the end of the arena and ran full tilt down the inside of the fence right in front of them.

Sammy's head swung fast as he followed the black blur. Then immediately he turned back to her. "Are you really going to get out there?" he asked, his brows bunched in concern.

Jolie bit back a laugh. After all she'd faced in her kayak, a few half-pint cows didn't scare her. Not that she'd dare tell Sammy that.

"You bet I'm getting out there!" she exclaimed. "It's fun. If you learn how to do it right, even small people can flip a steer." He didn't look convinced at all. "You can do it, Sammy. It's all in the technique."

"We're going in two groups," Morgan called. Joseph clamored over the rail and jumped from the top rung to the ground. Instantly five more boys bailed over the rails and sauntered to join Joseph.

Jolie sure hoped she still had it—she hadn't run

around an arena after a steer in years. It hit her that if she hoped to get Sammy to participate at all today, she needed to go in the first group and lead by example. She climbed the fence and dropped to the ground on the other side.

"No!" Sammy yelped, grabbing hold of her shirt sleeve through the railing as if he feared he would never see her again. "Please don't go," he implored her.

"It's going to be all right, Sammy. I promise. You'll see, sugar," she urged.

Adrenaline was flowing through her, a feeling she relished. She gave Sammy's hand one last reassuring pat, then pulled away. She had never let fear hold her back—until the accident. But today, there was nothing inside the arena that remotely frightened her.

Matter of fact, she felt more alive than she had in a long time. Pure fun was what she called this.

It had been too long.

With big, goofy grins, the boys were whooping and waving her over. She jogged their way, smiling.

"Count me in on this one," she called to Morgan. She rubbed her hands together, joining the boys behind the line that had been drawn in the dirt. Mentally she went over the names of the boys in the group—Joseph, Wes, Tony, Caleb and Micah, who was sixteen with rusty-brown hair, a lean face and eyes the color of well-washed jeans. They were all grinning from ear to ear as they looked at her.

Jolie clapped Caleb, the youngest, on the shoulder. "Hey, aren't you Mr. Braveheart," she teased, and his grin widened to touch his ears.

She was just starting to enjoy herself when she looked at Morgan. The man's scowl told her he wasn't happy with her at all.

So what else is new?

"You sure you want to do this? It's been a long time, and yester—"

Jolie cut him off. "I'm fine, and I'm sure. Let's get this muggin' goin'!"

"If she can ride those rapids, I bet she can mug a puny five-hundred-pound steer." Joseph grinned and spat a sunflower seed husk to the ground.

"Why, thank ya, Joseph," she quipped, gloating a little at Morgan.

He frowned at the teen. "Maybe you need to tend to your own business."

Joseph chuckled. "You sure been ornery the last few days, Morg."

"Yeah," Wes agreed. "Real grumpy."

Morgan's scowl deepened. "May I have a word with you?" he asked through bared teeth. Wrapping his hand around her biceps, he started walking her away from the group.

Once they were a good distance away from everyone he let go of her arm, leaving her skin tingling from his touch. She felt a rush of disappointment but wasn't sure if she was disappointed that she'd felt a tingle or that he'd removed his hand.

"I can do this if I want to, Morgan McDermott." Here was one of the problems that had prompted her to pack her bags six years ago—the man was pushy.

"You passed out yesterday. That's not like you. I've thought about it all night and I've decided that there must be something wrong. You going to tell me what that something is?"

I've thought about it all night. He'd had her on his mind—the knowledge sent a shaft of joy straight to her heart. She continued to glare at him, though, because she'd never liked his bossing her around. It was all coming back to her now. Once he'd put his ring on her finger, he'd started trying to dictate her life—tried to wrap her up and keep her safe. It was out of concern, but she was not a china doll and refused to be treated as one.

Even if she felt broken right now.

"I did not pass out. I got a little faint is all."

"You would have hit the floor like a rock if I hadn't caught you."

"Maybe, but—"

"Jolie, I'm not kidding. You come back here after all this time, and you aren't kayaking. You nearly died—yeah, I know you didn't elaborate on that, but Nana is my grandmother, so I'm informed. I know what a close call you had. I'm not blind and I'm not stupid, Jolie. There is something wrong with you and I want to know what it is."

The man was impossible. "It's none of your business."

He loomed over her, his scent filling her senses. "I'm responsible for everyone out here and if you have some kind of condition, I need to know about it. You were hired on to this ranch without my say-so, but guess what? That makes you my business, especially if whatever's going on affects your job."

So his interest in what was wrong with her was because she *worked* for him. There was nothing personal about it. Nevertheless, she caved under that blue-eyed stare, blurting out, "I'm having trouble sleeping ever since the accident. I'm having a few nightmares."

"Nightmares," he repeated, clearly startled. Then his expression softened. "I guess that's understandable after what you went through."

Jolie suddenly wanted to tell him more, but was aware that all eyes were watching them as they stood practically nose to nose. This wasn't the time or the place. And now that she thought about it, she didn't want sympathy from him.

"I'm dealing with it," she huffed, "which is why I'm taking some time off. Now, can we get this done?" she asked.

"Fine, do it," he snapped. "Only, and I mean *only,* if you're sure you won't be passing out and getting trampled."

"Such a sweet thought," she replied, syrup dripping from her words as she crossed her heart. "I promise."

She spun and jogged back to the boys. Energy surged through her—for now, she was alive and unafraid, and Morgan McDermott couldn't tell her what she could or couldn't do.

She gave high fives to the boys.

"Let's do this," she said before turning her attention to the midsize steers milling about in a huddle. She took them all in and zeroed in on her pick, a hefty black angus that had some challenge in his eyes. Sure, there were a few mild-mannered ones milling around, but she'd never taken the easy route.

"Just so y'all know, I'm in it to win it," she warned.

"Win it," Wes said in comical disbelief.

"Win it," she clarified. Their disbelief was all the challenge she needed. She'd always liked having something to prove.

"Here you go, hotshot. Be my guest," Morgan said, issuing his own challenge as he handed her a rope.

Jolie stuffed the tie rope in her back waistband and gave the guys a grin just to egg them on because they were looking at her as if she'd lost her mind.

"All right," Morgan commanded. "This is our version of a muggin' competition. All of you will go at the same time and first man—*person*—to get the steer by the horns and to the ground is the winner of this group. Once we have the winner established of this go-around, then one of you will tie its legs and be timed on that. We'll do the same with the second group, and the overall winner will be determined by time. Remember, we'll have a team roping in a couple of weeks and you'd better be practiced up on your roping and tying by then, because I'm bringing out the real steers." This information won huge grins and a ton of chatter.

"Everyone behind the line and we'll get this show started. Get set," Morgan called, "go!"

It was on. Dirt flying, steers running, cheers threatening to lift the roof off the building, Jolie and the five boys ran out into the arena. Jolie focused on her target—which was heading for Denver, by the looks of it. Anticipating his movements, she raced after him. When he spun, she dived for him—and landed face-first in the red dirt.

Sputtering the bitter, gritty dirt, she was on her feet in a flash. Hands out to either side, she waved the steer back when it would have broken left. Scrambling for traction, she broke right, then lunged again…and grabbed him.

"Gotcha, big boy," she grunted, locking her elbows around the steer's blunt-tipped horns. Instinct from years on the ranch kicked in. One arm locked around the horns, she grabbed the animal's jaw, dug her boots into the dirt and twisted the steer's head as she leaned back on her heels. Once she felt his weight shift she hung on, pulled harder and let herself fall back into the dirt. The steer came with her, landing on his side. Only then did the riotous yells and cheers begin to register.

Holding the angry steer's horns to her chest, she waited for someone to come tie its legs. A shadow blocked out the overhead light and Morgan grinned down at her.

"I reckon you haven't lost your touch after all," he drawled.

Looking up at him like this felt so familiar, like when they were teens and this was a normal part of their weekly routine. The steer squirmed, reminding her that she still had it by the horns. Thankfully Joseph raced up and had three legs tied in seconds.

Sliding from beneath its head, Jolie stood and dusted off her backside. "If you ask me," she said, her poker face in place as Rowdy joined the group, "that was kind of slow."

That got a grin from Morgan. She grinned right back at him, and for a moment the tension between them eased and she felt her heart pick up the pace.

Rowdy jogged up and nudged her arm. "Not too shabby, pest. For a girl."

"A girl who had her moments of glory beating you both a time or two."

"I'm impressed," Wes said, wiping sweat off his forehead with the back of his arm.

"You did it!" Sammy exclaimed, elbowing his way through the group and grabbing her around the waist, hugging her tight.

"Hey, I told you I would." She returned his hug. A warm feeling expanded in her chest like a hot air balloon, lifting her spirits. Beaming with gladness, Jolie met Morgan's hazardous indigo gaze…and *whoosh,* just like that, all coherent thought evaporated right there under the big lights.

Morgan was rocked by the attraction buzzing through him as he watched Jolie. It was as if they'd been swept back to the past and the world was right again.

He was also more than a little startled by the enthusiastic way Sammy had just latched on to her. His thoughts were stumbling all over themselves as her dancing green eyes locked onto his.

Clearing his throat, he tried to clear his brain and turned his gaze to the kid.

Sammy connected with Jolie on a level that he hadn't come close to doing with anyone else. Morgan could practically see the kid's heart on his sleeve. And it immediately reminded Morgan that—no matter what he'd been feeling toward Jolie just minutes before—her being here was a mistake.

Oh yeah, a big mistake—of gargantuan proportions.

The kid needed stability—he did not need to fall for Jolie, then have her exit his life in a few short months. But Morgan's hands were tied. Jolie was the kind of person who drew people to her—no doubt about it. What could he do now? It was clear that it was already too late—Sammy was attached with a capital *A*.

"Morgan, did you see Jolie?" Sammy yanked on his sleeve to get his attention, too young to realize that Morgan hadn't taken his eyes off Jolie for even a second while she was out there.

"I saw. She was born to be a cowgirl." His observation came out before he could stop it. Born to be a cowgirl riding a horse—and ended up riding river rapids. The thrill was clearly much more exciting out there taming white water in places he couldn't pronounce much less compete with.

"I learned everything I know from Morgan, so do as he tells you and you can't go wrong."

Her glowing eyes settled on him, drawing him like some poor moth to a flame. After all that had happened, he could still get lost in those gorgeous eyes of hers.

"Ha!" Joseph exclaimed, blessedly drawing Morgan's attention. "Morg taught me and you *still* beat me."

Jolie's laugh tinkled like wind chimes. "The steer has to cooperate, too, you know. That handsome hunk of a hairy dude wanted to be caught by me, I think."

"Well, duh," Wes drawled. "Who wouldn't?" That brought hurrahs from all and big goofy grins that were becoming commonplace around Jolie.

Jolie laid a hand on her heart and smiled at the boy. "Aw, that is so sweet."

She was a born dazzler. Morgan realized that in all of her wordplay with the boys, she'd still somehow managed to make them feel good about themselves, even though she'd beat them fair and square. He liked that, and appreciated it.

But what he didn't like was that he felt the shield he'd built up around his emotions slipping a notch as his admiration for her returned full force—he was feeling pretty dazzled himself.

Nope, he didn't like that. Not at all.

She hadn't even been back three days and he was already starting to think she was great again. He scrubbed the back of his neck, catching the half-amused eye of Rowdy.

Shaking his head, Morgan turned and headed toward the exit. While they prepared for the next groups muggin', he needed to put some distance between him and Jolie.

Some poor sodbusters just never learned.

Chapter Six

You can't go home again.

The words echoed in Jolie's head all the way back into town after the steer mugging. She'd never expected to come back to the sleepy little town she'd grown up in on that day six years ago when she'd hit the gas and aimed for the horizon. She'd left in a haze of confusion and tears, torn between two worlds. Now, here she was, amazing as it seemed, about to start teaching at Sunrise Ranch.

The boys on the ranch had instantly won a spot in her heart—and school hadn't even started yet. It felt as if she'd known them longer than two days. She was as attached to them as they seemed to be to her, and she knew it made Morgan edgy.

Everything about her made Morgan edgy, it seemed. But it sure had been nice to get a genuine smile out of him after she took down that steer. She'd felt that smile clear down to her toes. It had been hard to concentrate after he'd stalked out of the arena, but she'd done it and tried her hardest to convince Sammy to try, even saying she would go and help him, but he'd refused. She hadn't tried to force the issue—hopefully time would help him.

Time would hopefully ease the tension between her and Morgan, too.

Jolie pulled into the vacant spot in front of the three-story Dew Drop Inn. The old redbrick structure had originally been a dance hall saloon back in the 1800s. It had had a whole host of other aliases through the years, too, including funeral parlor, boardinghouse and restaurant. It was said to have welcomed many famous folks—and just as many infamous folks—inside its doors at one time or another.

It had been boarded up for years and fallen into terrible disrepair before Mabel Tilsbee bought it and poured her soul into it. And for over thirty years now it had been the Dew Drop Inn. Black porch posts held a second-story balcony, and Mabel kept two pots overflowing with ferns on either side of the ornate double doors with leaded glass insets and heavy brass fixtures.

Inside, wooden floors were covered with rugs that had been worn down over the years but still held a lovely charm and gave the place a welcoming feeling. For Jolie, the inn was home until she found a place to rent or decided to take the small house at the ranch Randolph had told her went with the job.

The decision was complicated by Morgan's being at the ranch, of course. She wasn't sure it was a good idea to be out there—around him—all the time, especially because it was obvious he didn't want her there. But even so, there had been moments—breathless times—when electricity crackled between them.

"Whoo," she whispered, just thinking about it. Even though Morgan had shut it down almost as quickly as it had happened, there was no denying they'd both felt it. And as a result, she was pretty certain he wouldn't

welcome her moving out there, encroaching on him all the more.

It was a dilemma.

Swinging her legs from the doorless Jeep, she paused to stretch her aching back—taking a steer down by yourself did tend to strain muscles—and take in the rest of the town she'd left behind.

It had just two main roads that intersected, and smaller tree-lined roads that led to old-fashioned homes with spacious yards. She remembered it as the Mayberry of her youth. The newspaper office was on the far end of town, along with the hardware store and the barber shop. A church bench sat on the sidewalk between the two businesses, where the older men of town gathered to fix all the world's problems. Chili Crump and Drewbaker Macintosh, whom she'd hugged at church that morning, were occupying the bench at the moment. In their mid-seventies, they'd taken the place of Snoot Pickens and Sargent Hanes, two characters who'd both passed but whose legends lived on in the tall tales of many.

A slight breeze fluttered over Jolie like whispers from years gone by. Yep, she was sure she'd been the topic of conversation on that bench many times—she could just imagine how it had been after she gave Morgan back his ring and hit the trail.

Poor Morgan. She hadn't really thought about what he'd had to endure after she'd broken their engagement. She'd mostly been thinking about her own pain, and her frustration that he couldn't support her decision to pursue her dream.

She swallowed, the breeze still whispering in her ears. Regret for the pain she'd caused settled like a rock in her stomach.

It was payback time—she was certain she was once

more the hot topic on that bench, and everywhere else in town. She'd prepared herself for that when she'd decided to come home. But giving them something to talk about was a small price to pay to make things right between her and Morgan, to apologize for hurting him—something she had to keep reminding herself she was here to do. Apologize and heal—that had been the plan, but the feel of his arms after she'd fainted had taken her off track and confused her reasoning.

She wondered how Morgan felt about being in the spotlight, which she was certain she'd put him in when she'd rolled into town. Folks meant no harm, but Morgan was a pretty private person who'd already had way more attention than he'd ever wanted, thanks to her… and Celia. If she had to guess, she'd say he was less than overjoyed that she'd come home and put him back in the hot seat.

Scanning the rest of the town, her eyes came to rest on the Spotted Cow Café. Vibrant red geraniums overflowed at the entrance, and the bright yellow door stood out like a welcoming beacon. She'd been the one who'd come up with the idea to paint the door lemon pie–yellow all those years ago. Jolie's stomach growled as she looked at it. Clearly, the door did its job, and did it well.

Behind her the string of bells on the Dew Drop Inn's door tinkled merrily. Jolie turned back toward the inn.

"Well, I'll be! If it ain't Jolie Sheridan! Hon, it's about time you came back home!" exclaimed Mabel Tilsbee, rushing from the building. The owner of the Dew Drop Inn engulfed Jolie and hiked her up in the air. Arms clamped to her sides and her feet dangling at Mabel's shins, Jolie felt her body shake in the breeze. Mabel had always had a soft spot for Jolie. She'd also been the one who'd told Jolie that she'd never be happy if she lived with regrets.

"I am so happy you're here!" Mabel cried as she squeezed the life out of Jolie. "Goodness gracious, this is the best surprise ever. When I got back into town a few hours ago and I found out you had checked in, I couldn't believe it!"

"It's good to see you, too," Jolie gasped, trying to move her arms. Mabel started jumping up and down—for a woman in her mid-sixties, she was as strong as a moose.

"Mabel, come on now, let the poor girl go," Ms. Jo barked from behind Jolie. Mabel obeyed her friend and released her. Feeling like a dishrag wrung dry, Jolie grabbed the porch post for support.

"Thanks," she wheezed. "I heard you were on a mission trip to Haiti."

"God was good to let me go. And good to let me come home." With her hands on her hips, Mabel stared at Jolie, grinning with her whole face. "Jo, ain't she a sight for sore eyes? I've been keepin' up with you," she said, not stopping long enough for Ms. Jo to answer her question. "And I saw that horrible accident. Just *terrible.* It was awful thinking of you trapped under that raging water. It's a miracle you're alive. A pure miracle, and don't you forget it. God's got plans for you, hon—that's what it is. Your shirt got caught under there on something, didn't it?"

Jolie nodded, her stomach turning over. It should have been a common roll maneuver that she'd made in the water thousands of times. But her shirt caught on a wayward limb beneath the water and everything went wrong.

Jolie's pulse grew shallow and she feared another fainting spell. It was maddening to feel so stinkin' weak.

"I'm thankful to be alive." She smiled and tried to put a good face on it, hoping they wouldn't see through her.

"And here you are," Ms. Jo said, her knowing eyes catching everything. "Home to have Mabel do ya in right here on Main Street."

"Hush," Mabel scolded. "I was just excited to see her."

"That'd be a reason to squeeze the poor girl in half."

Mabel hiked her chin, gave her friend a warning look, then returned her attention to Jolie. "So how are you? Jo told me you were having some problems from it."

Of course Ms. Jo would have confided in Mabel. Maybe she'd said something to Nana, too. Well, there was nothing she could do about it now.

"Some." She cringed. "You know, it was scary, I'll admit, and I, well, I thought it was time to take a breather." She looked from one friend to the other. "And the truth is, I'd been missing the place, and everyone…" Her voice trailed off.

Mabel nodded, her expression empathetic. "Jo told me you're working at the ranch. Land's sakes, that was a shocker! How's that going, you bein' out there and Morgan, too?"

Mabel never had been one to dance around the elephant in the room. She just walked up to it and grabbed it by the trunk.

"He looks fine—good as ever." Boy, was that ever an understatement! "He's not too happy to see me, as you can imagine. So how have you been?" Jolie asked. Time to change the subject.

"As ornery as always," Ms. Jo grunted.

Jolie chuckled. "You still keeping Nana and Ms. Jo in line?"

"*Phassh*—me being the ornery one? Those two are the ones who can't be kept out of trouble."

"That's exactly what Nana said about you," Jolie teased, thinking of her visit with Nana. She was sure that Nana had kept her two friends in the loop about everything after that visit, probably because they were all worried that Jolie was going to break Morgan's heart again. Of course the man had shields of steel up—his heart was in no danger whatsoever.

"Where's the fun in staying out of trouble?" Mabel asked with a smile.

Jolie chuckled—it felt so good to see her old friends. It had been strange growing up and not really knowing girls her own age. She'd had the boys at the ranch, and all these ladies—her mother's friends—whom she'd thought of as grandmothers.

A big white ranch truck rumbled into town and slid into the slanted parking space just in front of them. Nana smiled and waved out the open window, her navy eyes luminous in the early evening sunlight. "Hey, there, gals. Y'all ready? Hey, Jolie girl."

"As we always are, Ruby Ann," Ms. Jo said.

"We're heading up to weed the flower beds at the church. Come with us," Mabel urged.

"Yes, come," Nana said, bobbing her hot-pink straw cowgirl hat with a peacock-feather hatband that matched her eyes. "No sense spending the evening up in that room alone. And I brought snacks." Those were magic words, because even though her lean figure wouldn't show it, Nana was a master in the kitchen, rivaling Paula Deen with her mouthwatering concoctions.

"Did you bring that spice cake I love for my welcome-home gift?" Mabel asked, winking at Jolie.

Jolie's heart warmed at their inclusion, her mouth watering when Nana said that she had indeed brought the famed spice cake.

"Sounds like a plan to me," Jolie drawled, feeling happier than she had in a while. The only thing that would have made this moment better was if her mother were here, too. Her folks had moved closer to Houston a few years back, to take care of her grandmother, and she didn't see them very often anymore.

"No way am I passing on that cake and y'all's great company." She looked down at her dusty clothes. "I've already swum in the dirt today, so why not dig in it?"

"That's my gal." Ms. Jo took her arm. "Come on, then, let's get this horse to a gallop."

Clucking and yacking away, they piled into Nana's ranch truck and headed out. *Maybe you* can *go home again.* The thought jingled through Jolie like a catchy tune as she settled into the backseat with Mabel, who was eyeing the spice cake in the wicker basket on the seat between them, temptation dancing in her eyes.

They drove past Chili and Drewbaker sitting on their church pew, Nana tooted her horn.

"Honkin' at your boyfriend, Ruby Ann?" Ms. Jo teased, hiking a brow at Nana.

"Ha!" Nana declared, chuckling right along with the rest of them. "That Chili is barking up the wrong tree when it comes to this ol' gal. But I do love to tease him."

They broke into more chatter after that, and Jolie felt good realizing that after everything she'd been through and all the ways she'd changed, Dew Drop was still the warm, wonderful, welcoming place it had always been.

There was comfort in that, and despite her tangled thoughts about Morgan, Jolie settled in for an enjoyable evening with the girls. Maybe hanging with these wise friends would give her some much-needed clarity.

* * *

Monday morning arrived with the resounding confirmation that Morgan hadn't just dreamed Jolie was back in town and teaching at the ranch. Like a bad headache pounding on the back of his eyes, she'd stayed on his mind all night after she'd taken down that steer and won the heart of every boy on the ranch.

Even the grown-up ones.

It went without saying that he wasn't in the best of moods when he parked in front of the chow hall. As luck would have it, Jolie came striding out of the building, a cup of coffee in her hand.

Setting his resolve, he climbed from his rig and tipped his hat at her. "Mornin'," he said, taking in the excitement in her eyes despite the dark circles she'd tried to hide with makeup.

"Good morning. It's wild in there." She motioned toward the chow hall. "I thought I'd go get my head on straight before they show up."

The sudden need to pull her to him, to feel her pressed against his heart, again slammed into him, looking at those circles under her eyes. The woman needed some rest. She'd said she was having nightmares—how bad were they? Obviously bad enough to be damaging.

"Sounds like a plan. They'll be over there soon enough and then all bets are off for the day. If you have any trouble, I'll be in my office most of the day."

Her smile put a catch in his breath. "There will be no trouble. I promise—though I haven't taught since student teaching, I'm a whole lot less gullible. It'll be fine."

Giving him a wink, she headed down the plank sidewalk that ran the length of the chow hall. He just stood there, like a fool, unable to move.

At the end of the sidewalk, she stepped onto the

gravel, paused, turning, then gave a hesitant smile. “Thanks, Morgan.”

He watched her go, her long cinnamon hair loose today, swinging like waves of warm spice tea midway down her back.

His jaw tightened. It took him a minute to catch his breath and pull his gaze away. He was one messed-up cowboy—that was the long truth of it all.

The chow hall was buzzing as he strode inside. Excited conversations were easy to pick up on as he headed toward the buffet table—“Jolie” this, “Jolie” that. Their new teacher filled the airwaves.

Not only had she successfully beat Joseph in the mugging—something they all aspired to do—but they were also excited about her kayaking, just like he’d suspected. Yep, it was more than clear they thought she was pretty awesome.

But would they still think she was awesome when she headed off into the sunset, leaving them all behind, standing in the dust?

A sudden poke in the ribs halted his downward-spiraling thoughts. Turning, he found his grandmother holding a spatula in her hand.

“Those eyebrows of yours are going to grow together if they get any closer. And that frown is never a good sign this early in the morning.”

Morgan grunted. “Mornin’, Nana. It sure smells good in here.”

Nana’s cheeks were rosy red from the kitchen heat. Tilting her head to one side, she crossed her red-sleeved arms over an apron that proclaimed, *Cooked with love—so hug me!*

“At least you noticed.” A teasing undertone matched the twinkle in her eyes. “I wasn’t sure you were even with us. Saw you talkin' to Jolie out there. If her being back has got you this shook up, then I'm not sure you're going to make it till the end of the semester."

"Nana."

"No one *heard* me. Now, really, are you okay?" Her Texas drawl was thick as the syrup the boys were fighting over at the end of the buffet line.

"Just concerned for the boys."

"They're doing fine. Stop worrying." She looked over at Sammy and B.J., whose syrup tug-of-war had gotten a little out of hand. "We'll talk about this later," Nana said, then turned her attention to the boys. "Hey, fellas, hold your horses! Do y'all think that syrup is the last syrup on earth?"

The boys halted in their battle, blinking at Nana in confusion, still clutching the syrup bottle between them.

"Well, don't just blink at me like a couple of owls. Answer my question like gentlemen. Sammy, what do you think? Is that the last bottle of syrup on earth?"

The kid swallowed like he had a biscuit stuck in his throat. "I don't figure so."

"Ma'am," Nana reminded him.

"Ma'am," Sammy added quickly.

"And what about you, B.J.—what's your answer?"

The younger boy cleared his throat. "Ma'am, Ms. Nana, it probably ain't. Only it's the only one I see."

Nana put her hands to her hips and her lips twitched at the corners. "You are both right. There is a lot more syrup in the kitchen, so I don't think you have anything to fight over. Thank the good Lord for your blessings and share that bottle or you'll both be eating your pancakes with no syrup at all."

Sammy was the first to let go. "Yes, ma'am. Are you sure there's enough?"

Morgan patted Sammy's shoulder. "There's plenty, so no more fighting."

"Sammy started it," B.J. offered, dousing his pancakes. "But he's new and ain't learned we got it good here."

Nana met Morgan's gaze with grateful eyes. He knew that it meant so much to her to be here for these boys and all the others who'd come through the foster care program to live here with them. He felt the same way. But he had his work cut out for him with Sammy.

He had to get the kid acclimated to the ranch. Small things like fighting over syrup didn't bother Morgan. But struggling to fit in did. He'd seen the look in Sammy's eyes as he'd let go of the syrup. Fear laced everything the boy did. Something about Sammy seemed different, but Morgan just couldn't put his finger on it.

Maybe Jolie would be able to help with that. The notion struck him as totally counter to what he'd been thinking since she'd arrived. He was still worried about her leaving—more so since seeing how the boys, especially Sammy, had taken to her.

But he knew he had to ease up. Fact was, Jolie was here and there wasn't anything he could do about it. Except pray that she did more good than damage before she left—and that his heart was still intact when she went.

Chapter Seven

The week flew for Jolie. She and the boys settled into a routine, though it did take some getting used to. Jolie wasn't teaching just one or two subjects, or even one age group. She was teaching all subjects to sixteen boys in grades one through twelve, all at varying skill levels—even those in the same grade.

She had every available teaching tool at her fingertips, though, and access to whatever she needed. The purpose of the private school was to give these boys a step up when it came to academics. Some of them had had such terrible home lives before coming to Sunrise Ranch that they either hadn't gone to school much at all, or their grades were far below passing. Morgan's mother had dreamed of not only giving boys the opportunity to live and experience life on this beautiful ranch, but also to see to their spiritual needs and provide the chance for them to thrive in all aspects of life. The boys Jolie had gone to school with had gone on to become doctors, lawyers, businessmen, ranchers, rodeo champions—the list went on. There were even a couple of preachers in the mix, and a missionary, too. Lydia's vision had been a blessing in so many ways, and this week Jolie had gotten to experience it from the other side of the desk.

She was tired, but her spirit felt peaceful. She'd come to the decision that she needed to move into the farmhouse that Randolph had offered. Maybe if she settled into a real home for a few months it would help ease the nightmares and she could get some much-needed rest. Despite the lingering worry that Morgan might have a problem with her moving to the property, she was excited to make the move that evening.

Friday had come quickly. She was cleaning off the chalkboard prior to heading to the inn to grab her meager belongings. The creak of the front door had her looking over her shoulder, to find Morgan.

Immediately her pulse skipped as it had on the mornings she'd run into him briefly at the chow hall. Each time she'd been unable to gauge what was going on behind those deep blues of his.

Her nerves jangled, and it felt as though butterflies had taken flight in her stomach.

"Hey," he said, closing the door. He crossed the room in a few quick strides, coming to stand beside her desk with his hat in his hands. "Are you done for the day?"

The butterflies fluttered more. Morgan McDermott still had the ability to shake up her world. It was maddening—the man should be outlawed. Dressed in worn jeans and a loose turquoise button-up shirt with rolled-up sleeves showing off his corded forearms...Morgan was all cowboy.

"Yes," she forced herself to answer, trying to get her focus off just how handsome a man he was. "And I might add that my first week as teacher has been a success in my book. I *loved* it." She pushed on, ignoring the butterflies. "It felt so good reaching for ways to ignite those curious minds." Wrapping her arms around her waist, she tried to find the right words to express her feelings. "Your mother, she had such vision, Morgan. I'm just so glad to have this opportunity."

She thought she saw shock flash in his eyes, but the shield he seemed to wear when he was around her clicked into place almost instantly. Except for the mornings she'd run into him in the chow hall, he'd stayed clear of her since the mugging. The connection she'd felt between them—if only for a moment—had disappeared just as he had.

"I've heard from the boys that you are one cool teacher."

"Ooh," she cooed, giving him a teasing grimace. "I know it had to hurt you to hear that. Worse having to *repeat* it."

That actually won her a smile that tickled her insides—and suddenly she was remembering being kissed by Morgan.

As if she'd ever forgotten it.

She'd been kissed a few times over the years by the men she'd dated, but there hadn't been many, and their kisses had been like cola without the fizz. No one had ever appealed to her—or affected her—like Morgan. Her gaze shifted to his lips and her pulse paused. She leaned slightly toward him, drawn by an invisible cord.

"The boys expressed what I've been worried about from the minute I learned about this deal you and my dad worked out," Morgan said.

Jolie prayed for patience with capital letters. Looked as if there was no reason for her to be thinking about Morgan McDermott's kisses after all.

"Morgan, come on. This bad attitude..." She let her

words trail off. She'd had little sleep, leaving no patience for this.

"I'm just worried—"

She pinned him with a glare and cut him off. "I *get* that you are worried that I'm going to run off and they will feel abandoned. But I'm here to help them, not hurt them. I've signed a contract for the semester and I plan to honor that."

Clamping his mouth shut, he said nothing, instead absentmindedly tracing a finger across the front of her desk. Despite her anger, Jolie shivered, thinking of his fingers tracing her cheek as they had so many times, so long ago. When he glanced up at her, his expression was less guarded.

"Look, I'm sorry. I didn't come here to fight. I've been watching Sammy ever since the calf wrestling and I think you're helping him," he admitted.

Had she heard him right?

"I came to tell you that I'll do whatever I need to do to help you help him," Morgan continued. His amazing blue eyes softened—he was actually conceding.

"G-good," Jolie stammered. She thought about trying to apologize again, telling him that she hadn't meant to hurt him. But she knew he would only deny that she'd hurt him in the first place. "That's the way it should be. Our past, what happened between us—"

"Is the past," he said firmly.

"Yes. We should still be able to help these boys even though we once had feelings for each other and it didn't work out."

What else could she say? She'd just come up against one wall after another with him—he'd made it clear there was no sense in rehashing old history that he had no desire to revisit. So she stopped trying. For now.

They stared at each other as if both trying to figure out where they went from here. He raked his fingers through his black hair and she could almost feel the sensation on her skin.

Slapping his hat on his thigh, he nodded, then strode out the door. On the steps he turned back toward her.

"I hear you've decided to move into the farmhouse." Topic changed. "Do you need help moving?"

"No, I'm fine. I didn't bring much with me, and your dad told me it was semifurnished."

"Yeah, it should be okay to get you by till you leave at the end of the semester. If you decide you need help, call and I'll bring some boys over to lend a hand."

Jolie rubbed her temple, watching Morgan stride away into the distance. Oh, what a tangled web they'd woven.

She missed him. She'd not only given up her fiancé, but her best friend, too. Had she chosen the wrong road that day?

The question was irrelevant—she'd had to leave. She just wished it hadn't cost her Morgan's friendship. She'd hoped that coming here to apologize would give her back her friend.

A soft bump and then a creak sounded from the back storeroom. She headed to investigate and found the back door standing open. Someone hadn't closed it properly, she thought with a smile. Kids.

Deciding it was time to be practical—no more drifting back to the past—she locked up and headed out. She had a house to move into and a man to boot from her thoughts.

Good thing she'd worn her riding boots today.

"Guys! Hey…guys," Caleb huffed when he finally made it to the horse stable where the other boys were tending to their horses. "Sammy..." He paused, taking a deep breath. "I think Morgan likes Jolie!"

Joseph spun around, the cool-down brush he'd been using on his horse still in his hand. "Whoa, slow down, slick."

"Yeah," Wes urged, putting a hand on Caleb's shoulder. "Breathe, dude, before you keel over."

Caleb gulped air, feeling as if his eyes were going to pop out he was so winded. He needed to tell this, to make them understand!

"Now, what were you saying?" Wes asked after Caleb had sucked in a couple more huge gulps of air and calmed down a little.

"Okay," Caleb said slowly, looking around the group, trying to harness his excitement. "I was over at the school, and I heard Morgan and Jolie talkin'."

"And?" Joseph urged.

"And guess what? I think they used to have a thing."

"A thing?" Sammy asked. "What's a thing?"

"Yeah, what thing?" Wes asked.

Caleb grunted, impatient for them to get it. "You know, a *thing*. For each other. Back when they were young."

Caleb noticed Joseph and Wes look at each other all serious.

"You sure about that? Like, what did you hear?"

"Jolie, she said— She was talkin' to Morgan and said, just because they used to like each other and it didn't work out, that shouldn't stop them from helping us."

"Well, what do you know." Joseph crossed his arms and got that look in his eyes that told Caleb he was thinking something over.

"Swweeet." Wes grinned.

Joseph looked thoughtful. "You know Morgan's been

like a dad to us for a long time and he's never been sweet on a girl."

"Well, there was that woman we saw him with once in town." Wes hooked his thumbs in his belt loops. "We never saw her again, so I figure that didn't work out so good."

Joseph nodded. "Yeah, he never talks about anyone."

"I heard he got left at the altar or something one time and it gave him a broken heart," Tony offered. "I'm just sayin', you know, like, do you think it coulda been Jolie?"

"Naaah, she wouldn't do something like that," Wes scoffed.

"I wonder, though." Joseph's eyes widened. "I heard Nana saying she left six years ago, then I got here not long after she left. And, you know, back then we didn't see much of Morgan."

Caleb waved his hands. "I ain't much on knowing what love looks like. I can tell you that Jolie looked real sad, though. And well, Morgan, he kinda looked weird, like he'd just swallowed some nasty cough syrup. Then he told her that that was the past and it should stay that way."

Wes whistled. "This is good. I feel *romance* in the air."

"That'd be cool." Joseph's grinned at Caleb as all the other kids started talking.

"You mean like if they fell in love," Sammy said, looking weird, too.

"But," B.J. piped up, "you said Morgan wanted it to stay in the past and he looked all mad."

"You'd have to have seen Jolie, the way her shoulders were all hunkered down like she'd just lost the rodeo or something. She was sad. That's all I know, though, because I got out of there. Fast."

"Sounds good to me." Wes wiggled his eyebrows.

"Yeah." Caleb grinned. "I think it would be neat to see Morgan with a girlfriend. Oh! She's moving into the farmhouse, too, and Morgan said something about how it would be fine till she left at the end of the term."

"It'd be like having a mom," B.J. said.

Caleb heard the wish in his voice and knew what he meant. Morgan and his dad were like their dads—they were the ones involved in running the foster care program. The house parents were great, but they were more like grandparents than dads. It would be nice to have a mom around the ranch.

"Yeah, until mine comes back to get me," Sammy said. "I like Jolie."

Caleb felt bad for Sammy. They all knew his parents weren't coming back. He'd find out eventually, just as they all did. "Then it's done." Grinning from ear to ear, Joseph looked at everyone. "So here's what we're going to do."

Good. Joseph had a plan. He always did—the boys counted on that.

"What are we gonna do?" Sammy asked, and Caleb nodded because he wanted to know, too.

"Whatever it takes." Wes cocked an eyebrow at Joseph, who laughed.

"Yeah, that's about it. We're gonna make those two spend as much time together as possible." Joseph winked at Sammy. "Short Stuff, if you like Jolie, we're gonna make it so she sticks around."

Tony, who was tougher than all of them put together, frowned. "My sister used to love this old movie about some twin girls who did all kinds of stuff to get their divorced parents back together. I think my sis thought it would work on our parents. There wasn't any saving that train wreck, though."

"See, that's the thing. If Morgan fell in love with Jolie, then she might stay and we'd have a cool teacher. Maybe then she'd teach us to kayak, too." Wes had been talking a lot about kayaking. He craved adventure and wanted to ride bulls, only that was the one thing on the ranch the boys weren't allowed to do.

"You did good, Caleb," Joseph said, clapping him on the back. "Real good."

Caleb grinned, feeling as if his chest was going to explode. "You really think we can do this?"

Wes and Joseph hiked their eyebrows at each other before looking at the rest of them.

"We're gonna give it our best shot," Joseph said.

"And that's a promise." Wes had a twinkle in his eyes that meant one thing: they were going to have fun doing whatever it was they were going to do. That twinkle *was* a promise.

And hopefully it was a promise to get Jolie and Morgan back together so Sunrise Ranch could feel even more like a home, with a dad…and a mom.

Chapter Eight

Jolie eyed Salty, the black mare she was about to ride. She hadn't been on a horse in years and hoped she didn't embarrass herself.

"You sure are taking your time getting in that saddle."

Morgan walked up beside her looking all-too-good in his beat-up cowboy hat and checkered shirt. His jaw was scruffy with a five-o'clock shadow and there was some challenge in his eyes as he studied her.

"I'm about to climb up there. I'm just wondering if you could have given me a bigger horse to ride." Salty was huge—at least sixteen hands tall and very broad.

"She's a good horse. Not as salty as she used to be." His lips hitched into a grin. "You can handle her and you know it."

"If it's like riding a bike, then yes, I'll be just fine."

He turned serious as he studied her. "You look worn-out, Jolie. Are you still having nightmares?"

Lately, Jolie had been fighting hard against the urge to try to knock down the walls that Morgan had put up between them. She knew she *wished* there were no walls between them. Wished she felt free to talk to him. But would that be a mistake? If there was no wall she might fall for him all over again, and where would that leave her…them? But despite her uncertainties, when he looked at her with such concern, she knew she was fighting a losing battle to keep the wall up between them.

"I don't want to talk about that right now," she replied. "I'd like to hop on this horse and see if I still have what it takes to be a cowgirl."

"Uh, yeah—you're being a little too humble. You're a natural-born cowgirl and that doesn't ever leave a person."

She gave a discordant laugh. "My composure is a bit shaken, so that's all the more reason to hop on this baby and join this roundup. The boys were pretty persistent in getting me to come along. Sammy truly wouldn't take no for an answer."

"That's the reason he's sitting up there on Cupcake looking like he's about to toss his cookies."

She laughed. "Poor kid. The good thing is he's doing it, and that is a really big step for him. If helping in this roundup gets him to push himself, then I'm all in."

Morgan tipped his hat at her. "Good for you. Load up. You sure you don't need any help?"

The twinkle in his eye caught her off guard for an instant. Was he teasing her, or…flirting? Seeing the old Morgan for a second dumbstruck her. "I think I can manage. Do *you* need a helping hand?"

He laughed at her offer, shot her a wink and strode off with his cowboy swagger. Watching him swing into the saddle, a sigh escaped her. Berating herself, she jammed her boot into the stirrup, grabbed the saddle horn and hoisted herself up with ease. It felt like old times. A sense of excitement washed over her—this was going to be a good day.

Only after she grabbed the reins did she notice the

boys watching her. Maybe it was her imagination, but they'd sure seemed interested in her past on the ranch this week during class. They'd asked all kinds of questions, even some about kayaking. She'd been happy to have made it through those without falling on the floor again.

She'd been able to put off their push for kayaking lessons, but that wouldn't last forever—the boys wanted to learn. She hoped she could eventually find her way toward teaching them.

Along with all those questions came some about growing up on the ranch. Even though she hadn't told them everything, she had given them small peeks into her life. And her life on the ranch couldn't be explained without stories of Morgan. They'd been inseparable as kids, long before he'd noticed her as a teenager. Long before she'd begun to panic that if she stayed at Sunrise, she would never find out who she really was and what she wanted out of life.

Long before she'd fallen in love with the feel of conquering a raging river, and long before she'd made the mistake of falling in love with Morgan, threatening her dreams of seeing the world one river at a time.

The boys were definitely getting to her. There was no way on earth she could look at those grins and tell them she didn't want to hang out with Morgan all day. So she'd agreed to come, and now she was suffering the consequences by having to corral the pitter-patter of her heart when he was near. No doubt about it, she was wrapped tightly around their wily fingers.

Giving them all a thumbs-up, she was rewarded by a grin from Sammy. B.J. giggled and Joseph returned the thumbs-up, then tipped his hat, copying Morgan. The kid was determined to walk in Morgan's boot prints. Jolie couldn't blame him—Morgan was a good, good man.

"Let's roll," Morgan called. Jolie took a deep breath, and off she went to spend an entire day with Morgan. She just hoped her heart could handle it.

A couple of hours later, Jolie rode over beside Sammy and Morgan just as Joseph charged after a steer that had cut and run for the gully.

"Catch it, Joseph!" Sammy yelled, startling the steers around him and making his horse jump.

Jolie's heart skipped some beats but regulated when Morgan grasped the reins of Sammy's horse before she bolted.

"Easy, Sammy." His deep voice rumbled with gentle concern that pulled at Jolie's heart strings. "Don't go yelling like that and yanking on your horse's bit. You'll scare her. Okay, son?"

"Yes, sir." Sammy's knuckles were white as he clutched the saddle horn. "I got excited. I sure wish I could ride like Joseph."

"You will someday. But until you're more confident, you'll have to remember to take it easy when you're out here in the middle of a bunch of cattle."

They all watched Joseph racing through the tall grass and around scraggly mesquite trees in pursuit. Whipping his rope from the saddle, Joseph had his loop instantly twirling circles above his head as he chased the steer.

"He's really good," Jolie said, watching the rope land in a graceful arch around the runaway's head.

"Awesome!" Sammy exclaimed in a loud whisper.

"He's a natural," Morgan agreed. "Joseph took to cowboyin' like a duck to water. Kinda like someone else I know. She just had more duck in her than cowgirl."

Jolie tucked a stray strand of hair behind her ear as

she took his half-teasing, half-serious words into account. "Funny. But there is some truth in that."

He nodded. "Believe me, I know."

Better than most. Even though he didn't say the words, Jolie heard them loud and clear.

All morning she'd been glimpsing the old Morgan, but now his shields slid back into place.

"I guess you do," she said. It was all she could say, because they both knew it was the truth.

Their gazes caught, like magnets pulled to each other. Jolie wanted to say so much to Morgan—

"Are you gonna teach us to kayak?" Sammy's question broke the moment—and it was a good thing, too.

"I'm not sure, Sammy. Like I said in class I'll have to see how things go."

"What things?" he persisted. "Wes said it looked real fun. We watched you on the computer and it was cool."

It struck her that he'd said teach *us* to kayak. He was getting braver.

"It's very dangerous." She forced herself to remain calm. They were simply *talking* about kayaking, she reminded herself. She wasn't in the water, wasn't near the water....

She wasn't under the water fighting for her life, finding the thrill of the ride not so thrilling when she held it up against being alive.

Sammy patted Cupcake. "Wes said I was too much of a scaredy-cat to ride a rapid."

"That wasn't nice of Wes to say," Morgan interjected, his tone saying he wasn't pleased with Wes. "He's a lot bigger than you and he likes doing things that are risky. You have to do what's comfortable for you, Sammy. *Not* what someone else wants you to do."

"That's right," Jolie said, relieved that the conversation was heading away from kayaking. "We're so glad you wanted to ride a horse this morning and help with the roundup. However, if it was something you really didn't want to do, then we would have respected your choice."

Sammy looked serious. "My momma was going to buy me a horse when I got older—I mean, she's *gonna* buy me a horse. She's probably trying to get the money to do it right now. So—so I need to learn to ride so I can be ready."

Jolie didn't know what to say. Maybe his mother *had* told him she was going to buy a horse. And what right did Jolie have to tell him he might never see his mother again?

Morgan shifted in his saddle. "It's good for you to learn to ride. It will help you join in with the others. Now, ease on over to the outside of the left line and stay on the outer edge. That'll help keep the cattle moving forward and not out. If a stray busts loose, let Joseph or Wes handle it. Got that? Today, your job is just to get used to the saddle and the cattle."

Sammy let go of the saddle horn and took the reins. He nodded, looking intently at the cattle. "I'll try."

"You'll do fine. Just do as I ask and stay safe. Okay?"

"Okay, Mr. Morgan."

Jolie smiled at him. "I'm so proud of you, Sammy. You're doing great."

Sammy's eyes widened as if he'd never heard a compliment before. "Thanks. I've been praying about my fears just like you told me. 'When I am afraid, I will trust in you, O Lord!'" As he repeated the verse Jolie had taught him, he finished as if he were a fire-and-brimstone preacher. Jolie laughed and Sammy, grinning, tapped Cupcake with his heels and headed off.

Jolie watched him go, pride swelling in her as if he were her own child.

Morgan eased his horse closer to hers as they started moving with the cattle, keeping Sammy close by. "What's the real story on why you won't teach the boys to kayak?"

Jolie had known this was coming. She'd known it ever since she'd passed out.

"I have reservations about teaching them is all."

"I've figured that out. But something's going on here that isn't right. Like I said in the arena, you leave your career, you're having nightmares, you look like you haven't slept in months. You get faint at the mention of kayaking—yes, I noticed exactly what we were talking about when that happened. And now you avoid even talking about teaching the kids the very thing that makes you tick."

His expression had hardened as he spoke and his words were matter-of-fact. It was as if he had placed her inside a glass jar, and he was on the outside looking in without emotion.

She hated it.

And the realization that she hated it hit her like a cannonball.

"Like I told you, I'm having a little trouble."

"And?" he prompted. He'd always had a way of pulling the truth out of her if he wanted it.

"I'm afraid—" She'd no more gotten the words out when they heard shouting at the front of the cattle drive. Another steer had broken loose from the pack and was heading for the hills as hard as it could run. This time it was Wes who took off after it, his rope spinning in the air. Suddenly his horse reared straight up, then began bucking wildly. Wes dug his heels in and hung on. He kept his hand on the reins and fought to control the animal that had suddenly turned into a bucking bronc.

The second the ruckus began, Morgan spurred his horse forward, as had Joseph and Rowdy. Jolie knew instinctively what was in the grass before she saw the rattler strike out at the horse's legs.

It was *huge*—its head was as big as her fist!

The horse bucked far enough away that the snake missed its target. Morgan tugged his rifle from its holder and fired before anyone else could get close.

He didn't miss his target.

Morgan had always been steady with his aim and a sure shot, just like his dad and brothers. It was a known fact out here sometimes it took a bullet to protect the herd. Or the kids.

"Yee-haw!" Wes yelled. Getting his horse under control, he whipped his hat off and grinned as if he'd just won the bronc-busting event at the National Finals Rodeo. She remembered Wes mentioning he wanted to ride bulls, but it wasn't allowed on the ranch. Even though she completely understood why the ranch wouldn't put the guys in danger like that, she wondered just how good he might be if given the chance.

Morgan's gun was back in its sheath before the smoke cleared and Jolie breathed a sigh of relief, sending up a prayer of thanks. It had been a very close call. If Wes hadn't been as good a rider as he was, he'd have been on the ground with the rattler and things could have been really bad. Of course to him, it was all a great adventure.

She remembered being that way. Before.

Jolie let the idea of God's goodness and protection wash over her. She knew in her case He'd been there for her, but she still couldn't seem to let go of her fear. She wondered what it was going to take to find her courage again.

She rode up beside Sammy, who'd halted his horse and sat frozen, watching the scene play out in front of him.

"You okay?" she asked.

His smile took her by surprise. "That was *awesome!* Did you see that? Did you see how Morgan shot that snake?"

Jolie chuckled. "Yes, I guess it was pretty awesome."

In the distance Morgan put a hand on Wes's shoulder and grinned. Now that everyone was safe and sound, Jolie had to agree it was like a scene straight out of the movies. The way Morgan had charged to Wes's rescue—he protected the boys in his care as though they were his own flesh and blood.

He *was* awesome.

Snared by his gaze across the distance, her whole being seemed to hum. Her breath caught and she suddenly felt lost. Why had she really come home? Was it to apologize to Morgan? Or was it to find out if she'd made a mistake leaving in the first place?

And the biggest question of all: Was it possible that she was still in love with Morgan McDermott?

Chapter Nine

Morgan nearly had a heart attack when Wes's horse spooked. Standing there talking to the boy, he gave thanks that the snake hadn't bitten the horse, and Wes hadn't been thrown to the ground.

"That was some great riding you did," Rowdy told Wes. "You can be proud of that. No doubt about it."

"Yes, you can," Morgan added. "That right there shows why it's good to be prepared with your skills. And God had His eye on you, too. Don't forget that."

"I won't, sir." Wes's wolfish grin faded for a moment. "I was ridin' and I was prayin' at the same time." His smile popped back in place. "I was prayin', 'Good Lord, get me out of here!'" He chuckled as only Wes could, and the rest of them did, too.

After the excitement, Morgan didn't get to finish his conversation with Jolie. He and Rowdy split up, each riding the perimeters of the herd, away from the boys, watching for any other rattlers. When they made it to the last watering hole, it had been a long day. They still had a way to go, but the longest part of the drive was done.

The guys were tired and hungry and the cattle were thirsty.

Nana and her "truck wagon," as they'd named her version of the chuck wagon, were a welcome sight. The bed of the truck was rigged with all the essentials to fix a meal out on the range, and Nana also towed a barbecue pit behind the truck. This morning she'd started them off with a hearty breakfast in the chow hall, but they'd had only jerky and water in the saddle for lunch. The delicious smell of roasting meat and baked beans wafted through the air as Morgan dismounted.

"Want me to take your horse to the river for water?" Sammy asked. Morgan noticed he was riding with a little more confidence than he'd shown earlier. Riding all day could do that.

Morgan handed over his reins. "Thanks."

"I think Jolie's sick," the kid said, worry in his tone. "She didn't look like she felt good when she got off her horse. Caleb took it to the river for her."

Morgan looked up and saw Jolie trying to hide a limp as she headed toward Nana. "Thanks for the heads-up, Sammy. I'll check on her."

Sammy grinned. "*Yes!* I mean, good. That'd be a *real* good idea."

Morgan watched the kid lead the horses toward the river, a little confused but mostly amused by the kid's over-the-top reaction. Then he headed toward Jolie. He knew she'd bitten off more than she could handle today with this long drive. She was in great shape, no doubt about it, but there was a difference between riding a rapid and riding a horse all day. A shorter drive to start on would have been better. But she'd let the boys talk her into coming today, even knowing what it would cost her. The thought that she would do that for them—well, it did his heart good. Real good.

"Sore?" he asked, striding up next to her and grabbing a paper cup to pour himself some of Nana's sweet tea, which was a blessing all the way down.

Jolie cringed. "Just a little."

Nana clucked her tongue at her. "Honey, I'm not going to say I told you so, but I will say you're probably not going to be walking tomorrow. A long salty soak tonight might save you."

"Oh yeah," Jolie groaned. "I may soak all night."

Morgan's hand tightened on his cup. Laughing in the face of pain was pure Jolie—the Jolie he'd fallen for. He halted that line of thought and shoved it out of his head.

Massaging her thigh, she crinkled her nose, grinning at him. "There are just some muscles that are only used when riding a horse."

"Yup." Morgan fought being drawn to that grin with every ounce of strength he had. "But I have to say you've been a real trouper about it. Sammy's worried about you, though."

She clapped a hand to her forehead. "He saw me ease out of the saddle. I tried to throw my leg over the horn and hop off, but the leg just wouldn't cooperate. It was pretty pathetic."

Nana handed her the plate she'd fixed as they were talking. "Take this over yonder beside the river and hang your toes in the water while you eat. Take a load off."

Jolie took the plate. "I wanted to help you, Nana."

"You will do no such thing." Nana shooed her with her hands. "You've been doing your part all day. This is pretty self-serve for everyone and little work on my part. Now go." She shooed Jolie again. With a grateful look, she headed not toward the river but away from it, going to a stand of trees where the shadows of the evening settled.

Nana quickly stacked another plate high with brisket and beans and thrust it into Morgan's hands and ordered, "You go with her."

His boots dug in, drawing a stern look from Nana and leaving him no choice but to go. Crossing the grass, he caught some of the boys watching him.

"Enjoy," Rowdy said with a smirk plastered on his face.

Morgan didn't bother to reply to Rowdy's teasing—he was too focused on continuing his conversation with Jolie. She'd been about to tell him why she wouldn't teach the boys to kayak, and what exactly she was afraid of. He'd been thinking about it all afternoon.

Joseph crossed his path before he got to Jolie. The kid was fighting a grin and an odd glint lit up his eyes as he shot Morgan a thumbs-up.

What was that all about?

Continuing on toward Jolie, he caught sight of Caleb, so busy watching Morgan that he tripped on a log and fell flat on his face in the dirt. Jumping up, the lanky boy dusted himself off as he grinned at Morgan.

Something wasn't right here. They were all looking too...happy. Watchful.

He sat down beside Jolie, then set his glass of tea between them on the flat rock she'd chosen.

"I'm thinkin' Nana is right. I'm going to be in a world of hurt in the morning even with a salty soak."

Morgan stabbed a piece of brisket. "I'm sure you're used to being pretty beat up after a river run."

"So right," she answered, rolling her eyes as she

scooped up a small forkful of beans and chewed. "These are so good."

He watched her enjoying her food for a couple of stretched-out moments and suddenly he felt like a goldfish in a very small aquarium. Glancing around he caught the boys watching him, although they immediately became very busy when they saw him catching their curious gazes.

What was with all the watching?

Ignoring them, he cut to the question he'd been turning over in his mind all day. "You were saying, before Wes tangled with the rattler, that you were having some trouble and that you were afraid." Jolie didn't take the bait and start talking. Quietly he continued. "What are you afraid of, Jolie? What's got you so tied up in knots that you're struggling with nightmares?"

She toyed with the meat on her plate, finally expelling an exasperated breath. "Okay, I'm only telling you this because we used to be…good friends. And I know you're going to pester me till I tell you and even pull the boss card, if needed."

"Yup." His mouth lifted at the corner—she knew him too well. "Right on both counts," he agreed.

"So here it is—the ugly truth of it. I can't bring myself to get back into my kayak."

What?

She couldn't have startled him more if she'd slapped him. She'd lived and breathed kayaking from the day he'd first introduced her to it when she was twelve—she'd already been after him to teach her for a year. He knew how dangerous it was when the water was up and had refused to take her out, but she finally convinced him, and they'd played around with the small rapids during the dry season, when the river had been low and slow. He wasn't into crazy thrills—he'd used his kayak more for fishing—but he'd taught the kid a few things. Nothing fancy, because he didn't know anything fancy. And he warned her to steer clear of the rapids when the rains came.

The next summer when the river was up, she sneaked down to the water and experimented on her own. He'd been hotter than molten lava when she told him she'd taught herself how to roll—which was no small thing—and several other tricks of creek kayaking.

But what could he do? There had been no stopping her. She'd had no fear of the water and she'd felt invincible.

Until now.

Staring into her clouded eyes, he realized he'd not had any idea how badly her brush with death on that river in West Virginia had affected her.

He studied her face. "I knew it was bad," he said, quietly. "But to make *you* afraid of the water? I can't grasp that."

She gave a humorless laugh. "Yeah, unbelievable. The girl you couldn't keep off the water is now afraid to go near it." She released a heavy sigh and rubbed her temples. "I can't get things straight in here. My head is so messed up. I'm in jeopardy of losing my sponsors if I don't get back out there soon."

Like the quick snap of a whip, anger ripped through him. "Don't they understand what you've been through?"

"I'm a professional. They pay me to compete with their logo on my shirts. I'm a billboard to them, and when I'm not on the water or doing press for an upcoming competition, they're not getting their money's worth out of me. It's understandable."

"*Understandable?* Yeah, I understand. You nearly died! They should have some sympathy for that."

"They do, to a point. I have to be back by Christmas, ready to shoot a commercial and test a new kayak for my biggest sponsor. We have to leave the country to shoot it in a warm climate, so they have to start making arrangements."

He had to admit that her life was interesting. She grew quiet, staring at the river that was just barely visible from where she'd chosen to sit. "If you're afraid to get in the water," he asked gently, "how are you going to train?"

"I'm still weight training, and I run each day before work."

"But you have to be in the water. You have to stay conditioned to it." Even he knew that jumping back in without being sharp would be suicide.

Jolie put her fork down. "I'm not sure if I'll ever be able to get back in the water, Morgan. I—I *lost* something when I was pulled under and I couldn't come up. I left part of me down there. I've had close calls before—that's part of the sport. This, this was different. It's like I lost my heart beneath the water."

Her eyes were huge, haunted. And he reacted on instinct as much as anything else when he slipped his arm around her shoulders and tugged her into hug. She responded by laying her head on his shoulder. "It's going to be all right, Jolie. Coming here, getting away from everything was probably a good idea. Distance sounds good to me."

It hit him that he could run with this. If he wanted her

back in his life, then he could milk this for everything it was worth—and get her to stay here on the ranch.

His own thoughts startled him. Did he want to do that?

He still had feelings for her—he couldn't deny that any longer. He might have buried them deep, but right now they were pounding at the steel plate encasing his heart.

Could he finally have what he'd wanted six years ago? Could he talk her out of trying to go back to life on the water?

His conscience pricked. This wasn't the way he'd want to be with her, no matter how tempting the option was. It wasn't honorable, and that was what he'd promised God he would be.

"It's going to be all right. You're the toughest girl I know, and I've never seen anything keep you down or hold you back."

She straightened, lifting her head off his shoulder. "Thanks for believing in me. I'm just not sure if I want to continue." Her beautiful green eyes shimmered. "I came back to reevaluate my life. And I'm not sure, Morgan, but I think I might have made a mistake when I left here six years ago."

A *mistake?* Morgan stared at her, shaken by the emotions richocheting inside him. His heart pounded as he tried to form a coherent string of words. None came. She *thought* she'd made a mistake when she'd handed him back his heart—did she get that? Did she get that she'd been holding his heart in her hands when she'd held that ring?

He shot to his feet. "I have to check the horses," he

managed to say with reasonable calm. Then before he could say anything stupid, he strode away.

There were moments in a man's life when the best course of action was to keep his mouth shut.

This was one of those moments.

Chapter Ten

Jolie's words were on Morgan's mind the rest of the week. After she'd dropped her bombshell, he'd gotten as far away from her as he could get.

And he'd stayed clear ever since.

Actually, he'd stayed clear of pretty much everyone. Because there were times a man couldn't hide how angry he was.

Four days after the drive, his dad met him coming out of his office.

"All week you've been about as ornery as that stallion we sold last year. What's bothering you?"

"You brought her here," he snapped, scowling at his dad. "What do you think?"

Randolph raked his hand through his hair in frustration. "Look, I know this is a tough situation. Nonetheless, I'm trusting God that it'll work itself out."

"That's mighty good of you," Morgan grunted, feeling no better for his father's answer. *He* was the one who'd done this to him; *he* should be the one to fix it.

"Morgan." His father's voice stopped him as he started to leave. "You're going to need to forgive her, you know. For *your* sake."

Morgan kept on walking straight to his truck, started it up and drove. He just needed to *go.*

Forgive her? His dad had no idea what Jolie had said to him. She *thought* she might have made a mistake. A *mistake!* So, what if she hung around here, he let her back into his heart and then—boom!—she realized that the water was pulling her back? Where would that leave him?

Right back where you were when she left the first time.

After what seemed like forever, he ended up at Tucker's office in Dew Drop.

His brother had chosen to run for sheriff after his tours of duty in Afghanistan with the marines were done. There wasn't much happening in the tiny town, but there was still a need for the law since the county was fairly good-size. He had several deputies and Tucker led them well. He was steady as a rock and the brother Morgan went to when he needed good solid advice. Rowdy was more reckless—and the last thing he needed right now was reckless. Morgan entered the sheriff's department and went straight to Tucker's office, knocking on the open door. Tucker was pouring himself a cup of coffee. "Hey, Tucker, got a few minutes?"

His brother grinned and held up the pot. "You are right on time. Want a cup?"

"Do you have to even ask?" He walked in and took a seat in one of two hard-cushioned chairs. Tucker filled two black mugs and handed him one before taking his seat behind the desk.

"How's the situation going out there?" he asked, not one to beat around the bush.

Morgan knew he meant Jolie. "Is it that obvious why I'm here?"

Tucker hefted a shoulder. "You have that deer-run-over-by-a-semi-truck look. But then again, I'm trained to be observant." He waved at the wall of credentials behind him and gave Morgan a wiry grin before taking a sip of his coffee. "Talk to me before you explode."

Morgan told him, in confidence, some of what Jolie had revealed to him. He needed Tucker's black-and-white view on things. Even before he'd gone into law enforcement, Tucker had always had a clear view of the world around him.

"That's a tough one," Tucker said, a slow whistle escaping him. "It must have really messed Jolie up if she's thinking that way. Trauma has a way of cutting deep. Changing a person."

Tucker had experience with this—he'd seen lots of action on hostile soil and lost comrades during an especially brutal attack. He had a slight limp from the bullet that had sent him home, and scars that he didn't talk to anyone about. Not even Morgan.

"She's scared and she's not sleeping well. Still, when the boys aren't asking her to teach them to kayak, she's herself. Well, almost. But I don't know if I can—or want to—try again."

Tucker nodded although he didn't interrupt.

"But if I did, I could talk her straight into thinking quitting was the thing to do. Tucker, this fear could guarantee that she stay here on the ranch."

"Sounds like it." Tucker's brows met over serious McDermott blue eyes. He frowned. "You'd have it made."

Morgan set his coffee on the desk, stood up and crossed to the window, where he stared out at the main street in Dew Drop. From here he could see the Spotted Cow Café on the corner. When they were teenagers he'd bought plenty of pie there just so he could tease

Jolie while she worked. She'd loved it. Life had been perfect then. He'd believed they had a future stretching before them.

"I'd be lying if I said the thought wasn't flip-flopping around in my head, and that'd be pretty pathetic." He swung around as Tucker let out a gruff laugh.

"Yup. So what are you going to do? No, what do you *want* to do?"

Morgan's eyes narrowed. "Hey, you're supposed to be giving me some advice, not acting like a shrink."

"You're doing fine on your own. So?" Tucker pressed.

Morgan shook his head, hating what he was about to say. "She needs to get back in that water or she's going to regret it for the rest of her life."

"I agree. Sounds like she needs help from a friend."

Was he that friend? Dropping his head, Morgan felt his chest squeeze tight. When he looked up, he met Tucker's watchful eyes. "That water is what took her from me in the first place."

"Yeah." Tucker's eyes shadowed and he seemed lost in thought for a moment. "Life comes in circles sometimes. This might be rough."

Morgan just nodded, letting the truth settle in on him.

"You can handle it. Morgan, she came back here for a reason. She could have gone to her family in Houston, but she came here. That says something to me." Tucker looked down into his coffee cup for a few seconds, and then back up at Morgan. "When I was out there—when things were at their worst and I thought I was going to die before anyone could get me out—all I could think about was coming back here. Coming *home.* It wasn't just the ranch. Don't you get it, brother? Jolie came home. Maybe she doesn't even know why, but she came. Give this to God and see where it goes.

You only live once. Maybe you need to take a chance and have no regrets."

Morgan knew Tucker was right. But that didn't mean doing what he suggested was going to be easy.

In fact, it was probably going to be the hardest thing he had ever done in his whole life.

Days had gone by since the cattle drive and Jolie felt at loose ends since Morgan had walked away from their conversation. The boys had tried several times to get her to join in on other activities with Morgan, but she'd always managed to have something else to do, enabling her to make an honest excuse. The last thing she wanted to do was make Morgan uncomfortable again.

It hadn't taken any gifts of discernment to figure out he hadn't liked what she'd said. The man had jerked to attention and stampeded to the farthest corner away from her—and he'd stayed there.

She didn't blame him really. She was confused herself. She hadn't even meant to say what she'd said—the words had just come out, like they had a will of their own.

But it had just felt so right, sitting there with him like old times. There had been such comfort in being with him, in telling him what she was going through.

And then she'd gone too far.

Exposed too much.

Well, at least now she knew that her being back at Sunrise Ranch hadn't softened his heart to her at all. It was good information for her to have.

So this morning, she decided she'd throw herself into teaching to distract herself, and it was the perfect day for it—it was science day, and she was teaching the boys how to make a volcano.

"A volcano!" Sammy exclaimed when Jolie told them what they were going to do.

Not ever having taught science—or ever thought she would have to teach science—Jolie had been a little intimidated by the subject. But she was actually enjoying the class. She told them they were going to build the volcano with just a two-liter bottle of diet soda, sand and water. And they jumped right in, sculpting the wet concoction around the bottle, which not only resulted in the volcano but in a few muddy teens as well.

After it dried, Joseph poked it. "Hey, that does look good. I hear they just foam a little, though."

"That's why we're going to add these candies to the soda. I read online that it will make things a little more exciting," Jolie said with a wink.

"Really? What's it going to do?" Sammy asked, intent on the project. He'd become Jolie's personal helper, and the happiness it seemed to bring him helped her heart.

Smiling at them, she opened the Mentos candy. "Now, I'm ready to show y'all what happens when these two chemicals are combined."

"Let 'er rip!" Caleb yelped. He was so excited to see the eruption that he could hardly hold still.

"Stand back, everyone," she said, looking around the room. If anything, they all crowded closer.

Wes backed up, giving her a wink. "Bombs away!" he called.

Joseph gave her one of his thumbs-up and chuckled, "Let 'er rip."

The younger kids giggled with glee as she poured the entire tube of candy into the mouth of the volcano. It erupted instantly—spewing everywhere! Foam and gunk hit the ceiling and splashed down on everyone. Jolie yelled and the boys whooped in delight.

And at that very moment, Morgan strode into the classroom.

"What is going on?" he yelled above the laughter of the boys.

"It exploded, Morgan! Look!" Sammy yelled, pointing at the ceiling and wiping liquid from his face.

Morgan looked up just in time—a glob of foam fell right smack in the middle of his forehead. Eyes flaming, he wiped it off with his shirtsleeve and glared at her. And with good reason. The room was a mess.

He'd avoided her all week, so why had he picked *today* of all days to show up?

"I thought the volcano was supposed to spew a *little,*" she said. "I had no idea it was going to erupt like Mount St. Helens."

Just great. He was going to give her the worst-teacher-ever award. She knew this just made him think of the mishap during her student teaching.

Hair dripping, she looked around the room. The boys stopped laughing and watched her warily, as if worried she was about to cry. She took in their expressions, and suddenly Jolie couldn't help it—she laughed.

Yes, she might look like an inept fool to Morgan, but this *was* funny. She laughed harder. The kids looked at Morgan and to her surprise, his lip twitched and then he, too, began laughing. And then the boys joined in.

When the laughter died down, Jolie slipped her arm around Sammy's shoulders, giving him a hug. "Now we have to clean up this catastrophe."

"We'll help," Caleb offered.

Jolie grabbed paper towels and began wiping the sticky soda from the computers. Thankfully, she'd had sense enough not to set the volcano too close to them and the soda had only splattered on the keys.

"So, were you trying to trump your classroom adventures as a student teacher?" Morgan's voice was warm with teasing and his eyes warmer as he looked at her. But the tingle that raced up her spine was the warmest of all.

"Just trying to keep things interesting."

He chuckled. "Always."

She stopped scrubbing computer keys and he stopped wiping the desk. Funny how that simple word affected her—*always*. What would *always* be like with Morgan? She'd given that up with him and yet she'd never stopped thinking about it.

Standing with him so close, feeling the warmth of him and smelling the scent of his woodsy cologne, she began wondering full throttle about him, about feeling his arms around her and his lips against hers....

Great, Jolie. Just great.

"You almost missed all the fun, Morgan." Joseph broke into her daydreaming.

"Almost," Morgan drawled, looking at Joseph. "Thanks for inviting me to come to the show. It was a bit more exciting than you'd said it was going to be."

So that's why he was here.

"If your teacher would read her instructions a little more closely, maybe things wouldn't get so crazy."

"That would be boring!" Sammy defended her, and everyone agreed. "I didn't even jump when that foam blew out of there," he continued, big eyes beaming and smile flashing.

"And that's saying something." Joseph gave him a teasing push on the arm. "You're comin' around, short stuff."

Goodness, Jolie loved these boys. In just a short few weeks they'd dug deep into her heart as if they'd been in her life forever. How had that happened?

This feeling must be embedded in Morgan even more deeply, she realized.

"Well, I guess I'd better get back to work," Morgan said, making no move to go as his gaze latched on to hers again.

She felt breathless.

She also felt the boys' full attention on them. Morgan must have, too, because he broke for the door, snagging what was left of the volcano experiment on his way out. "I'll toss this in the back of my truck and put it in the Dumpster. Unless you want to use it again." He held it toward her with a half grin.

She smiled. "You might want to save it. That volcano will probably become part of Sunrise Ranch legend. It could be valuable someday." When he chuckled, she said to the boys, "Clean up a little more, fellas. I'll be right back."

And she followed him outside.

Morgan tossed the volcano in the back of his truck and then turned to face her as a soft breeze sent wisps of hair splaying across her face. To her surprise Morgan lifted his hand and gently brushed them off her cheek. A wave of emotion made her heart race and suddenly she was thinking about kissing him…and wondering if he was thinking the same thing.

His eyes darkened as he caressed the strands of her hair between his fingers. Butterflies fluttered inside her chest—no one had ever made her feel the way Morgan did with just such a simple touch.

"I better go," he said suddenly, letting go of her hair and reaching for the door handle. "Hold it down in there," he added with a wink, then climbed into his truck and drove away.

Jolie didn't move as she watched him go. She was unsure exactly what she was feeling…but it felt like hope. Could it be that there was a chance for them? Was she crazy to even think it?

As she turned to head back into her classroom, she was startled to see the windows full of grinning faces.

Unless she was mistaken, she wasn't the only one wondering if she and Morgan had another shot at love.

Morgan entered the stable, on his way to take a look at the new foal. It was quiet and sunlight filtered in through the windows, giving the stalls a glow.

The foal was a beauty. He was lanky—all legs with a sleek body that promised one day to be a beautiful cutting horse. If he was as talented as his daddy, they might have another champion on their hands. Rowdy had won the title on the foal's daddy two years in a row.

"He's looking good, isn't he?" Rowdy said, coming from the barnyard.

"Yeah, he looks just like Pep." Pep's bloodline was famous and a good building base for the ranch.

"Good ol' Pep, he knows how to mark 'em. Now if we could just get a few of his colts with some of his talent, we'd be in the money."

Though Rowdy grinned, Morgan knew he was serious. On a ranch the size of Sunrise, they pursued multiple avenues that could generate revenue as well as give the ranch a reputation for quality in every way. It also gave the boys exposure to different aspects of ranch life, and different possibilities for their future.

"Jitterbug's going to do us proud. You know he is," Morgan said, hanging his elbows over the stall gate next to his brother.

"He'll do. So, how's it going with Jolie? Y'all sure were looking cozy at supper during the roundup."

"We were just talking."

Rowdy studied him. "You going to throw in with her again? Forgive and forget and see where it goes?"

Morgan studied his boots. He'd almost kissed Jolie. But he was a grown man with responsibilities—he needed to have a clear head, and he wasn't sure he could do that around her.

Tucker had told him to give it to God and have no regrets.

Today he'd been tempted to do just that.

"I'm just asking," Rowdy said when Morgan remained silent. "I'm not sure I could do it in your situation. I like Jolie—always have—but that was harsh the way she led you on like she was going to marry you and then the minute she got the offer to join that kayak team, she jumped ship and bailed. My question is, can you ever trust her again?"

Bingo.

Morgan rubbed his jaw—startled by Rowdy's unexpected advice. Instead of being reckless it was on target with Morgan's thoughts. "She's here to teach the boys and work out a few issues she's had since the accident. I'm not going to kid myself into thinking she's sticking around this time. I'm not throwing in with her."

But I am going to help her get back in the water.

Rowdy slapped him on the shoulder. "Be careful."

"It's under control, but thanks for being in my corner." Morgan hadn't thought Rowdy was in his corner, and it felt good to know differently.

"What are brothers for?" With that, Rowdy sauntered out of the stable and disappeared into the bright sunlight. Morgan turned back to the foal.

Can you ever trust her again? Rowdy's words echoed

in his head—and his heart. Truth was, he couldn't. He didn't.

And that was the answer he'd been searching for. The attraction was obviously still there, but without trust, it didn't matter.

He was going to help Jolie get back in the water because it was the right thing to do. But it didn't mean he'd give her his heart on a platter again.

Morgan had a good life and he'd come to enjoy it. If it got lonely sometimes, so be it, because finding a woman to share his life had proven to be more trouble and heartache than he ever wanted to risk again. First Jolie and then Celia—though truth be told, Celia had hurt far less than Jolie. Still, he'd opened up to both of them, bared his soul and let them into his life—and they'd both left.

Nope, Morgan wasn't ever going to trust a woman with his heart again.

He would help Jolie, and ensure that she moved on at the end of the semester. And it would be the best thing for both of them.

Chapter Eleven

Gulping air into her burning lungs, Jolie leaned forward and grasped her knees. She'd been doing sprints for thirty minutes and was covered in sweat, her muscles on fire. She'd let herself get out of shape in the month since she'd arrived at the ranch, and now she was paying for it.

Straightening, she wiped her brow with her fingertips and continued to breathe heavily. The hill she stood on was steep—pure torture, and excellent for a workout.

She smelled the sweet scent of pure country air. It was hot air—even though it was now September, the temperature still hovered in the low nineties—but it was Texas country, her country, and she'd missed it.

She hadn't told Morgan the whole truth last week when he'd asked her how she was staying in shape. She'd exercised a bit, but not like she needed to in order to be in ultimate physical condition to hold her own against the rapids. Her endurance had to be in top form. If it wasn't, it could mean life or death.

Embarrassed by her half truth, she'd begun a rigorous exercise routine the very next day. She'd needed to work out her frustrations over how Morgan raced away from her when she'd told him she thought she'd made a mistake in leaving six years ago. That the workouts helped her to feel more like herself was an added bonus.

The feel-good endorphins were definitely working their magic, and she needed them. Until today, she'd thought there was no hope for Morgan and her. But standing beside his truck earlier, he'd thought about kissing her—she'd seen it in his eyes. And she'd thought about kissing him. Thinking of that moment sent shivers through her.

Heading through the woods toward the farmhouse, she made herself think of everything she had to be thankful for instead of thinking about kissing Morgan. Being alive was top of the list, and coming home to the ranch, and meeting the boys. And Morgan was up there, too.

Since she'd been back, Jolie realized a bunch of things, including the fact that she'd felt adrift even before the accident, as if caught in a backwash. What had driven her for so long had come to mean less and less, and things she'd put on the back burner had begun to tug at her.

In the beginning of her career, it had been different. Driven by the need to conquer as many rivers as possible, she'd been hard to stop in those first four years. Regrets over how she and Morgan had parted always trailed her, but her desire to be the best female professional kayaker in the field overshadowed her regrets.

Not so these last two years—things had begun to change. When her friends and competitors began slowing down, getting married and beginning families, she'd become restless. And sad. It took two for her dream of a family to become reality. Her love life had dwindled to almost nonexistent after she gave up dating, which had been nothing but disappointing. And she'd begun to really regret her past…and regret hurting Morgan.

After the accident, she'd known she couldn't run from it any longer. She'd told herself she was coming here to make amends, but now she knew she was here for more than that. Much more.

So here she was, her entire life in flux, so full of unrest that she was confused. And so full of longing, she was toying with fire.

The white wood and cheerful red shutters of her house came into view through the trees. Nothing fancy, but homey. And after being on the road so much, homey was exactly what she needed.

Stepping onto the back porch, the loud rumble of a diesel pickup signaled she had company. Going to investigate, she rounded the corner just as Morgan got out of his truck looking tall, dark and dangerous for her heart. Jolie sent gravel flying skidding to a stop.

She knew after a workout in scalding heat that she looked like a red lobster. Still, her pulse jumped despite her sweaty self.

"Jolie," he said, his eyes moving over her, probably taking in just how terrible she looked. "I was on my way to check some mares close to foaling and the boys told me I should see if you wanted to go." He grinned. "Just for the record, *I* thought you might want to come, too. I know you used to love the baby crop."

Jolie clapped her hands together. "Oh, Morgan, I would love, love, *love* to see the babies—are there any running around yet?"

"A few." He chuckled.

So the boys had sent him, but Morgan had thought it was a good idea. If she'd been wearing any boots, that fact would have just about busted them clean off her feet. "I'm a mess. Can you wait while I change?"

"You're fine. I mean—"

"Are you kidding? *I* don't want to be closed up in a truck with me right now, so I'm pretty certain you wouldn't want to, either. Give me ten minutes. Okay?"

"You got it." Following her to the porch, he sat down on the old wicker rocker that had been there when she moved in. "I'll be right here," he said, looking up at her with those blue troublemakers. Jolie almost tripped over the doorstop.

Her mind going wild, she raced into the house. Morgan had come for her. Heart pounding, she made quick time in the shower, not even giving the water time to warm up. Then she proceeded to sling clothes all over the place in search of the right thing to wear. The clock was ticking when she finally decided on the fourth shirt she'd tried on, along with the second pair of white shorts. Slipping her feet into her sandals she hurried to yank her wet hair into a ponytail, put on some moisturizer, a hint of mascara. Finally she gave herself a nod in the mirror, noting the tint of pink from the sun.

Or was it from being flustered?

With a minute to spare she raced from her room and ran hard into an end table with her knee. *Ouch.*

Through the screen door, she glimpsed Morgan fingering his Stetson between both hands, studying the hat like it held the secrets of the universe. Her heart clutched as he raked a hand through his ruffled hair and took a deep breath.

Was he nervous?

The very idea sent a tingle zipping through her. It was a good feeling to know she wasn't alone in this.

"All done." She pushed open the door, forcing herself not to sound too breathless, too eager. "Ready if you are."

Who am I kidding? she thought when Morgan looked up at her with those perfect blue eyes. *I'm not ready for this. I'm not ready for this at all.*

"Great, let's get this show on the road," Morgan said, jumping up from the chair. A little shaky in the knees, he caught the scent of her freshly washed hair. Whatever she'd used made him dizzy it was so sweet.

Get a grip, he told himself. He was in trouble and he knew it. Better to get this over with. He turned and headed for his truck, then remembered his manners and hurried back to open her door for her.

"I am so excited," she said, looking up at him like she had at the school the day before. Her eyes were so luminous he could practically see his fool face in their reflection.

He gave a stiff smile and put his hand on her elbow, assisting her into the truck. His fingers tingled as he touched her soft skin. Hurrying back around the truck, he slid behind the wheel. He'd never been happier that truck manufacturers had started making trucks bigger—he needed as much space as possible between him and Jolie.

Driving down the lane, the trees hung over the paved road like a canopy. It was a beautiful, sun-dappled section of road that he loved. And apparently so did Jolie.

"I've always loved this part of the road. When I was in Kauai, I saw a road with magnificent canopy over it. It's been painted and photographed an unbelievable amount of times. Every time I drove it, all I could think about was this little stretch of road in Texas and how much I'd loved it."

He glanced at her. "I didn't know there were any rapids in Kauai."

She shook her head. "I was there for a promotional event. My sponsor also makes rafts and wanted shots of me on the Na Pali Coast rafting. I *loved* it there—it was so gorgeous. And I got to swim with dolphins—one of the cool perks of my career."

"It sounds great." What else could he say? She certainly wasn't going to get that kind of perk here on the ranch. All the more reason to be cautious. In the end, he was certain Jolie would pack her bags and go back to the life that took her all over the world and let her swim with dolphins.

"It *was* great," she said. "And yet, Morgan, it's so good to be home." Her voice wavered slightly. They cleared the tree canopy, turning into the drive that led to the mares. When they stopped, she quickly pushed open her door and hopped down, as if to get away from what she'd just admitted. "Let's see these mommas and their babies."

Sliding from the truck, he followed her to the fence where she studied the mares and their rounded forms.

"They are beautiful." She pointed out some of her favorites, talking a lot about each one. She was as nervous as he was, he realized. "You always did have a great eye for a good horse."

They were standing close again, as if drawn to each other. "Thanks," he croaked, his nerves getting the best of him. "It's just a talent God gave me."

"Well, we all have different talents. Yours is definitely cattle and horses."

And hers was riding a river in a plastic banana, as Rowdy always called her kayak.

"You have a wonderful talent with the boys, too, Morgan. They love you so much." She turned so that she was facing him, leaning her shoulder against the wooden fence post. The sunlight sparkled off her drying hair in a way that he liked.

"I try." It was the truth—he really did. "We've had some great kids come through here. I thought about leaving a few years ago, then decided instead to take on more responsibility and become involved. It's been a blessing to me."

In more ways than he could ever tell her. When his life had crashed around his feet after she'd left, he'd jumped into his relationship with Celia too quickly. After that had fallen apart, he'd almost left Sunrise. But deciding instead to be more involved with the ranch had been a turning point in his life, and the only way he could describe it was to say that he'd found his calling.

And now he would help her get back to *her* purpose in life so that he could continue on with his own. Maybe even take a chance on love without being on the rebound this time.

"And you've been a blessing to them," she said, breaking into his thoughts. "I think of Sammy and how lost and alone he must have felt when he came here. But you and this ranch, and Nana, and Randolph and Rowdy and everyone here...you're rebuilding his life, and the lives of all the boys. You know that, don't you? You're putting a new foundation of love beneath their feet." Her voice broke and it touched his heart.

He couldn't speak.

"Morgan," she said, her eyes brimming with sincerity, "I have to thank you for letting me stay. I love being a part of all this." When he still didn't say anything, she turned back to the horses and pointed at a very pregnant chestnut mare. "I predict she's next. What do you think—tonight?"

He forced himself to disengage from her and look at the mare. "I might have a good eye for horses, but you're the one who always had the eye for due dates. We'll see if you're right. I'll have Pepper bring her into the stalls just in case."

Opening the gate, he led the way into the pasture. Jolie spent the next little while patting and talking to all the mares. Morgan stilled his heart against how much he loved seeing her with the horses on Sunrise Ranch. He reminded himself that this was not her dream.

"Oh, what a sugar you are," she said, laughing when a gentle bay tried to nibble at her ponytail. Each mare she talked to got some sort of encouragement along with a gentle, loving touch of her hand.

It made Morgan more jealous than he wanted to think about.

About ten horses later, he realized visiting the mares had been a bad idea. Clearing his throat, he decided, purely for self-preservation purposes, that it was time to talk about getting her back in the water.

"Can we go over there to that tree? I'd like to talk to you about something."

Curiosity lit her eyes. "Sure. Lead the way."

Pushing old memories from his mind, he led the way to the tree, checking for snakes before letting her sit. She placed her palms on the trunk behind her and leaned back to study him, her lanky legs crossed.

"Shoot. Tell me what's on your mind."

"I want to make you a proposition."

"Oh really? And what would that be?"

Dinner and some stargazing.

"I want you to listen to me before you jump in."

Cocking her head to the side, her eyes narrowed. "Sounds a little sketchy."

Morgan sat beside her. "I've been thinking about what you said, about being afraid of going back in the water. And also that you may have made a mistake when you left."

She inhaled a shaky breath and looked away.

"Jolie, I'm going to be honest with you. I don't want to get into whether your leaving was a mistake or not. I've moved forward—things change." Her shoulders stiffened. "But what I do know is that you've never shied away from a challenge. Fear has never defined you. If you don't get back in that water, I think you will regret it for the rest of your life. And you can't live with regret like that."

Jolie blinked several times, looking solemnly at him. "You know, it was fear of regret that drove me to leave all those years ago."

"Yeah," he forced himself to say. "And I understand that now. I'd be lying if I said it hadn't hurt back then. But you did what you had to do. And now you have to do it again."

She looked at her hands and then into the distance before finally looking back at him. This evasiveness wasn't like her, which gave him more insight into what the accident must have done to her.

"I've been thinking. Soul-searching. I'm not sure I want to continue kayaking."

"That's just fear and you know it," he said. "What about the guys? They are going to hound you until you teach them, you know."

She bit her lower lip, thinking. "I can't talk to them about the accident."

"All the more reason to just get back in the water and do it. Where's the girl I knew?"

She gave a humorless laugh. "I don't know if you've noticed but I'm not that girl anymore, Morgan. I'm almost twenty-eight years old."

"I've noticed." Oh yes, he had. "Look, you couldn't have kept up your competitive edge if you didn't still have the drive that you had before."

"Maybe I *don't* have that edge or that drive anymore. Maybe that's the problem. Did you think of that?"

"I don't believe it," he said gruffly, not liking the defeat he was hearing. "Not you."

She stared at him unsmiling. Seconds ticked by.

He fought off the urge to pull her into his arms and tell her that he would keep her safe. "Here's my proposition," he said instead.

A furrow appeared between her brows. "Shoot."

"I take you to the river and we work on your getting back in the water. No one has to know. We can get you over this hump and on with your life."

"Why are you doing this?" Anger tinged her words.

"So you can help the boys. And get back to the life you love."

Her eyes flashed. "You just won't believe—"

"No, I won't, Jolie," he snapped, losing patience. "You're afraid. And I don't want you here just because you're afraid."

Now he'd done it. The truth was out and he couldn't pull it back. Well, so be it.

She stiffened. "I see." She stood up and paced a few feet away from him. With her hands on her hips, she kept her back to him as she contemplated her situation. Finally, she swung around about as angry as a wildcat. "I'll do it, for the boys. I'll show them that letting fear keep you down isn't what we do. That God will help overcome. I just hope He gets with this program soon."

"That's okay with me." He knew she was still hot at him but holding it in check.

"So, when does this start?" Her hand was on her hip, her chest heaving with anger.

Feeling drained, he stood. "How about tomorrow afternoon? The boys have chores after school, so that's a good time to get away. I'll pick you up around four, if that works for you."

"Fine." Jaw clenched, she turned and stalked back across the pasture.

That was his cue—the conversation was over. She was not happy with him, but at this point, he didn't care. He was doing what needed to be done. Because the sooner she got back in the water, the sooner she got out of here. And the sooner she got out of here, the better it would be for both of them.

Chapter Twelve

The sound of the rushing water set Jolie's nerves on end. Before the accident, it had made her adrenaline pump and her energy level skyrocket. Now she was terrified by the sound, and by the thought of stepping into the swirling water and climbing into her kayak.

She'd had to push her anger at Morgan aside this morning so she could teach class. But last night she'd fumed at the high-handed attitude he'd had when making this proposition. For him to *assume* he knew what was best for her was irritating beyond comprehension—he didn't have a clue.

Okay, to be fair, he *was* right about the fact that the boys would hound her until she was forced to tell them the truth, and she didn't want to admit she was afraid. Especially not to Sammy—what a hypocrite she would be. So that was why she'd finally agreed to do this.

Before the accident, Jolie had really been afraid only once in her life, and that had been the day she'd handed Morgan back his engagement ring and driven away from him. God had given her the strength to do that—to reach for something more in her life, to dare to go beyond the boundaries of what was comfortable.

God was going to have to give her the strength to do the same here.

Only, right now she felt nothing except the cold edge of panic. Palms as wet as if she'd been dipping them in the river, her heart racing with anxiety, she marched down the path behind Morgan.

What am I doing? The question echoed in her mind.

Fighting came the answer, pricking at her like a thorn.

Jolie hadn't faced the possibility that her real reason for taking a break from kayaking was fear—it was easier to make it about needing to set things straight with Morgan. But the idea that Morgan could be right about her fear *bothered* her. More than she wanted to admit.

She was scared spitless, as Chili Crump would say. Both he and Drewbaker had fought in two wars and yet they both said crawling off in that yellow banana she rode over waterfalls would scare them spitless.

Long ago she'd thought they were just teasing her. Now she understood exactly what they'd meant.

"Are you all right?"

Morgan stopped a few feet ahead of her. She hadn't even realized she'd halted in her tracks until he'd turned around.

They were on their way to the spot where he'd first taught her to kayak.

"I'm fine," she lied, catching up to him.

It wasn't as if she was the first person this had ever happened to. Her friend Rita had gotten tangled upside down a couple of years ago and hadn't come back to the sport yet. She was a ski instructor in Colorado and guiding white river rafting expeditions in Tennessee. At least she was able to get on the water in an eight-man raft. Jolie hadn't so much as gotten her big toe back in the water.

"You don't look fine," Morgan said gently, studying her face.

So much for his not seeing her terror. Tears were welling way down deep, threatening to surface.

"Come on, talk to me, Jolie. Tell me what you feel. It didn't used to be hard for you to talk to me."

"I'm fine." She passed him on the trail. "I really am." *Liar, liar, pants on fire.* Her heart pounded, threatening to explode.

"No, you're not," he snapped, storming toward her, eyes blazing.

"Morgan McDermott." She swung around, glaring at him. "Stop telling me how I feel." Angry at herself for being a wimp, and at him for forcing her to do this, she lashed out. "How *dare* you!"

Tramping down the path, she could practically feel Morgan breathing down her neck. Despite her defiant spirit, her steps faltered the closer she came to the water, and her knees weakened. Her mouth went dry and her stomach hollowed out.

Crazy. This is crazy...and embarrassing. When she came to a sudden halt, Morgan slammed into her.

Grasping her arms, he kept her upright on the steep incline. His touch tempted her to throw herself into his arms, to bury herself in the security she knew she would find there.

Instead she forced herself to continue toward the sound of rushing water.

You don't have to do this! the wimp inside cried out to her.

Right. She was finished with kayaking anyway, wasn't she? Teaching full-time was the new plan. So she didn't have to be bullied into this. Panic gripped her like a choke hold and she spun, intent on fleeing.

Instead she found herself pressed against Morgan's hard chest, looking up into his dark eyes so full of concern.

"Whoa, take it easy," he urged, his tone softer than she'd ever believed possible.

Shaking her head, she backed away from him as though he was a hot frying pan.... The rest of the saying slipped her mind as his hands wrapped around her arms and his calm eyes searched hers.

She had to tell herself to breathe or she'd have suffocated right there as Morgan gazed into her very soul. "I—" *Breathe.* "I'm going back. I don't need to do this. It's ridiculous." The rush of the river seemed to get louder. She pulled away, trying to free herself from his grasp, but he held on tightly.

"Jolie, you can do this. Come on, babe. You can." His voice was full of compassion. "I know what happened to you must have been horrifying. But I also know you, Jolie. You can overcome this."

Swallowing cotton, she shook her head. Humiliation was the worst. Blinking fast, she fought off tears. *Please, no crying!* She hadn't cried at all since the accident—she'd held it at bay, even at its worst. Now a tear slipped from the corner of her eye.

The tenderness on Morgan's face made things worse. The pad of his thumb brushing the salty drop aside did her in as the tears she'd refused to cry for so long began to spill from her eyes, one by one.

"Don't cry, Jolie," Morgan said tenderly.

"I'm not," she denied.

His eyes twinkled but he didn't laugh. "Whatever you say."

She dropped her head to his chest and flat-out lost it.

If Morgan hadn't already figured out the seriousness of Jolie's situation, he clearly knew it now. Jolie wasn't a crier. He'd seen her get dragged and stomped by steers that would make a man cry, and she'd only gotten mad. She might look delicate, but she was cut from tough stuff. The fact that her sobs were soaking his shirt and her shoulders trembled in his hands shook him to his core.

"I'm sorry, sugar. I didn't mean to make you cry." He gently placed his hand on her head and stroked the length of her silky strands. "You don't have to do this today."

As she rested her head on his chest, he was certain she could feel his heart thundering away.

"No," she said in between sobs. "You're right, I need to do this, but as mad as it makes me…I can't…seem to make the last step into the water. I can't even make it *to* the water." Her eyes sought his. "I honestly think I'll pass out before I get my toe in the water. Isn't that a twist?"

Even though the last words were an attempt at humor, there was nothing funny about the situation. "If you make progress every day, it will happen."

"What will? Me passing out?" She attempted a grin.

He didn't. "No. You'll eventually get in the water, and then get in the kayak…"

She took a deep breath, finally getting a handle on her tears. She nodded, the hint of a smile still quivering on her lips. Morgan's heart stopped and every cell in his body went on alert as he stared down at her. She blinked—once, twice—and her lips parted. He felt her heart quicken against his own.

"Morgan." It was a mere whisper and it drew him like honey as he lowered his mouth to hers.

Instantly the years slipped away and it was just like it used to be between them. He hugged her close, wanting to feel the warmth of her against him. When her arms slipped up and around his neck his knees nearly crumpled beneath him.

Trouble. The tiny word wedged its way into his head.

This was supposed to be all about getting her back in the water so she could leave to pursue her passion, passion that wasn't for him.

She will *leave. She has to.*

Pulling away, he heaved a breath as they stared at each other. The world slowly tilted back into place. "Are you feeling better?" he croaked.

A twinkle lit her eyes and he was glad he'd helped put it there, if nothing else.

"How could I not be?"

He found himself pushing her hair behind her ear, his fingers lingering, sliding down to her nape. She trembled at his touch and it took every ounce of his strength not to lower his lips to hers again.

"We'd better get back. We'll do this again tomorrow if you want—I mean, we'll try to get you in the water. Not—" He shut his mouth before he said anything else.

"Yes, you're right. If I'm ever going to be able to look at myself in the mirror again, I need to be able to conquer this. Tomorrow is a deal."

"No, wait. We're taking the boys out to build fence right after you let them loose tomorrow. I forgot." Understandable that he'd forget—his brain was fuzzy after kissing Jolie.

"Sure," she said, moving a step away from him. "I remember the boys mentioning that. They asked me to come along. I told them I graduated from fence building a long time ago."

Morgan chuckled, seeing that just the idea of not having to get in the water tomorrow was a relief to her. "You never thought you'd be back here teaching, either."

"True. But believe me when I tell you that stringing barbed wire in hundred-degree weather is *not* on my bucket list."

He wanted to ask her if kissing him again was. Afraid of her answer, he kept his mouth shut.

They headed back down the trail, and he talked sense into himself the whole way while clanging warning bells continued to go off in his head. They'd kissed once, and based on the way he'd reacted, he knew it could never happen again. Because if it did, he was a goner for sure.

Chapter Thirteen

"Aw shucks, Jolie, do we have to learn to cook?"

Jolie had to fight the urge to scoop B.J. up in a big hug. "Cooking is a skill that even boys need to learn."

"We'd rather be ridin' and ropin'," Sammy groaned, trudging along beside B.J. They were trailing the rest of the boys, making their way across the pasture toward the chow hall.

"You'll both live. Nana, Ms. Jo and Mabel are excited to teach you. I want you two to be nice to them and appreciative of the time they're spending to do this for you."

Sammy squinted up at her in the sunlight. "You been tellin' me not to lie, Jolie. If I tell them I'm likin' it, then that'd be a big fat lie."

Jolie almost fell over in a heap of laughter.

"Me, too," B.J. added. "I ain't but eight. Don't that make me too young to fiddle with a stove?"

Anything to get out of cooking or baking.

"Believe me when I tell you that you will be well supervised." Both boys' frowns practically dragged in the dirt under their feet.

Nana was holding the door open for them when they

finally got to the chow hall. "Well, boys, glad you could join us," she said, a grin in her voice.

"Do we have to do this, Nana?" Sammy asked, as if he was going to get a different response from the one Jolie had already given him.

"Yes, you sure do, little man. And by the time we get through today, I bet you'll both be the fried egg kings."

"Eggs," Sammy said in dismay. "You mean we ain't even cookin' cookies?"

"'Aren't' cooking," Jolie corrected. She was his teacher after all.

Nana hooted. "You're cooking pies *after* you learn to cook something that'll actually put nutrition in your system."

Meeting Nana's laughing eyes, Jolie shook her head in dismay. "The other guys seemed excited about coming. I thought that was a little surprising, but these two, they take the cake."

Nana hustled them along toward the kitchen. "The other boys have been through this before and know we have a good time in the kitchen. These two ruffians weren't here last year."

Jolie thought back to when she'd gone to school on Sunrise Ranch. "We didn't cook when I was here."

Nana dipped her chin. "Randolph wouldn't hear of it. Thought it was for girls. That man." She shook her head and rolled her eyes as if to say he'd been stuck in the dark ages. "I've since changed his mind. I convinced him that many of these boys might have to cook for themselves one day and need to know the basics. And, well, then he saw firsthand with his boys. Not a one of my grandsons has a wife to cook for him yet and I had to help them all out with what goes on in a kitchen. You'd have thought those handsome cowboys had two left hands when it came to knowing the first thing about working a kitchen."

Jolie got a comical image in her head of Morgan elbow-deep in dishes with pots overflowing and the stove on fire. "I struggled a bit myself when I went off to college." She chuckled. "My poor mom didn't think I was ever going to eat anything except cereal and power bars."

The gloom hanging over Sammy's and Jake's heads was almost visible as they trudged into the kitchen several steps ahead of Nana.

"What in the world is wrong with you two?" Ms. Jo demanded in her no-nonsense voice, a twinkle in her eye. She had her fist on her hip, her gray head cocked to the side and a get-your-attitude-straight look on her face. Jolie grinned.

The boys were young but they came up to Ms. Jo's shoulder. When they didn't smile, she whipped her crooked pointer finger out and hiked her brow at them. Jolie knew they were in a heap of trouble—trouble that would be good for them in the long run.

"I didn't just ask that question to the air, boys. We're going to have ourselves a mighty fine time in here baking and cooking, so I'd surely like to see a little enthusiasm. You only get out of life what you put into it."

Sammy's eyes were big as saucers. "You ain't gonna whip us, are you?"

Ms. Jo's thin brows practically banged together and her eyes flashed with indignation. "*Whip* you? Why would I want to go and do that? I know for a fact that once you dig your fingers into the pie crust I'm going to teach you to make, you are both going to want to bake pies for a living because you're going to have so much fun."

"Fun. Cooking?" B.J. looked far from convinced.

Joseph had already tied an apron around his midsection and came striding over, his ever-present grin on his face. "Come on, little slowpokes, get your aprons on and let's get this show on the road. I'll show you my skills from last year."

Ms. Jo winked at the cute teenager. "Now that's a great attitude. B.J. and Sammy, right?" she asked and they immediately nodded. "Y'all go with Joseph here and he'll get the two of you all set up. Do you trust me?" B.J. nodded instantly, but her question clearly startled Sammy. His expression was guarded. "Trust is something earned, son, and I'm aiming to earn your trust so remember what I've said. Deal?"

Sammy thought on it. "Deal," he finally said. There was no doubt in Jolie's mind that Sammy would be watching everything Ms. Jo did. And when it was all said and done, he'd have a verdict.

And a very tasty pie to call his own.

Who knew cooking could build trust in a little boy who really needed a good experience in that department? As they walked off, Ms. Jo pivoted to her. Nana and Mabel, who'd been across the room handing out aprons, came over to join them.

"So, how are things?" Ms. Jo asked without so much as a blink of the eye.

"Things?" Jolie pretended ignorance.

"Now, Jo, easy does it," Nana chuckled.

"Easy does it, my foot," Jo balked. "I've been waiting for a little news and haven't seen hide nor hair of her."

"That makes two of us," Mabel harrumphed. "And I've had to put up with Jo's constant complaining because you've been AWOL. It's enough to make an old woman crazier than she already is!"

Jolie laughed. "Y'all knew exactly where to find me,

so don't think I'm feeling sorry for you." She hoped the boys would return and they'd have to turn their attention to the baking at hand, but the boys were fighting over who was going to have to wear the apron with the big strawberry on it, and there was no telling how long that was going to go on. "I haven't been AWOL. I've been working."

Ms. Jo's brow cocked. "Is that all?" She sounded suspiciously like she wanted something more than that to be going on.

"Yes, that's all. And exercising—keeping my training up takes time, too."

"And going on roundups and birthing colts, too."

Nana was not helping the situation.

"Sounds like fun to me," Mabel cooed. "It is so romantic on the trail—once you get past the dirt hanging in the air and the heat. And the sweaty horses. On second thought, maybe the trail isn't a place to foster a budding relationship."

"Budding? Who said anything about a budding relationship?" The words were out of her mouth before she could clamp a hand over the traitorous lips—she hadn't intended to talk to them about any of this at all. "The last time I checked, you three were all against my starting anything up with Morgan." The words were hissed quietly so that the boys wouldn't overhear.

"True," Ms. Jo said. "However, there have been a few indications that maybe we were a bit hasty being protective of our boy."

"We're all set," Joseph called.

Praise the Lord for the intervention!

Joseph and Wes had lined up the motley crew like they were about to compete on the *Iron Chef* television show.

Jolie grinned. "Look, ladies, the boys are ready to cook."

"Bake," Ms. Jo corrected.

"Cook," Nana said, giving Jo the eye. "Eggs and sausage are necessities."

Ms. Jo gave a snort. "Depends on who you ask."

"Then I guess it's both bake and cook," Jolie chirped, escaping from the interrogation huddle. She had a terrible feeling that things were just about to start heating up.

The thing was, she hadn't seen much of Morgan since their kiss. They'd agreed to meet again and attempt to get her in the water, but it hadn't happened. She'd gone home and immediately gotten cold feet. Obviously Morgan had, too, because he hadn't called yet to reschedule the date. And that had been fine with her.

At least she'd kept telling herself it was fine. But just thinking about the feel of his arms around her and the heat of his kiss made her cheeks warm.

So far the only good thing that had come of the day beside the river was that her nightmares had eased up. And that was probably just because thoughts of Morgan were keeping her from sleeping in the first place. But that was a piece of info that she and she alone was privy to. And she planned to keep it that way.

Morgan was late. On purpose.

"You better hurry up," Rowdy teased as he threw a leg over his horse and jumped to the ground, his spurs jangling on impact. "We don't want to let the pies get cold."

Morgan deliberately took his time getting out of the saddle. When Nana overheard the boys begging him to come join their cooking class, she'd basically demanded that he and Rowdy sample the food with the boys. He'd groaned, knowing full well that the boys had an agenda—they were always trying to get him and Jolie in the same room. Knowing he was going to have to face Jolie for the first time in a week scared him.

He'd arranged his every move over the last few days with the sole purpose of staying out of her range. And with good reason. She was far more dangerous to him than he'd ever suspected. He'd naively thought that what she'd done to him would insulate him from the feelings that he'd had for her; he'd thought his heart would be protected. And then he'd gone and kissed her.

And completely messed up his world.

One wrong move and he was mincemeat.

Rowdy was having a lot of fun teasing him. The slug was supposed to have his back, not enjoy watching him hotfoot it across coals without his boots on.

"Payback is going to be sweet, just you wait, little brother."

"Hey, I don't have anything on the burner right now, so don't get your hopes up." His lips curved into a lazy smile.

"I wouldn't get too smug if I were you," Morgan warned, striding past him. "I'm a patient man."

Rowdy's chuckle followed him as he headed toward what he was certain would be a circus—with him as the main attraction. He knew Nana had keyed in to the fact that he was avoiding Jolie. She had asked him a time or two where he'd been hiding out at lunch—he might as well have admitted his guilt flat out. All the more reason for her to join forces with the boys to get him here today.

And she had backup—Ms. Jo and Mabel would be watching his every move, expression and twitch.

He was doomed.

And Rowdy wasn't helping him at all.

The last thing he needed was everyone in that room

realizing what a vulnerable spot he was in. A rock and a hard place would have been better than this—at least he'd have had somewhere to hide. But no such luck.

Steeling himself for what was to come, he shot the good Lord a plea for help, pulled open the door and stepped into the center ring under the glaring spotlights.

"Morgan, look what *I* did!" B.J. yelled, instantly alerting Jolie and everyone else that Morgan had entered the room.

"Hey, I'm here, too," Rowdy clowned, pretending to be hurt, following Morgan into the kitchen. The room seemed to shrink with the two tall cowboys in it.

The instant Morgan's gaze sought out Jolie, all the air disappeared. Jolie dropped her metal spatula on the stainless-steel worktable, splattering meringue everywhere—including on Sammy—before it clattered to the floor. Every eye turned her way.

"You kinda like him, don't you?" Sammy whispered, blinking through globs of fluffy white meringue on his eyelids.

Jolie gasped, as much from having splattered the kid with pie topper as from his keen observation. "Why would you say that?" she whispered, concentrating on cleaning the sticky stuff from his face with the skirt of her apron.

He squinted as she held his chin. "'Cause you get all nervous when he's around. That's what happens in all the gushy movies."

"No, I do not like him." She scrubbed harder.

"At all?" Sammy asked, looking confused now.

Guilt slid over Jolie. She stopped her scrubbing so she

could leave some skin on the poor kid's cheek. "Yes, I do like Morgan. As a friend," she added quickly.

Nothing more.

"Well, you're pink right now and they do that in the movies, too, when they like the guy a lot."

She was about to ask him when he had time to watch all these gushy movies, but Morgan was coming their way.

"B.J.'s pie looks great. How does yours look, Sammy?" he asked, his eyes landing on her for only a moment before turning to Sammy. She wondered what was going on behind those pools of blue as her pulse cartwheeled through her body and memories of his kiss played havoc on her senses.

"We're about to put it in the oven. See?" He proudly pointed at the chocolate meringue pie. He'd been helping Joseph and finally decided to make his own, so they were running late on getting his into the oven.

"That looks mighty tasty." Morgan placed his hand on Sammy's shoulder. "You did a fine job."

"I didn't want to at first. You know cooking ain't for boys. But Nana showed us how to cook egg-and-sausage breakfast tacos so us boys won't starve when we go off to college."

Morgan chuckled. "She taught me the same skills before I went off myself. It came in real handy. And pie making—now that would have really come in handy for a college man."

A grin spread across Sammy's face. "I liked it. Jolie helped me and she did good. Till she dropped her spatula when you came in." He leaned toward Morgan. "And she turned kind of pink. You know what that means, don't you?"

Heat stung Jolie's cheeks. "Hey!" She gently tugged on Sammy's ear and he laughed mischievously.

"You tell me what it means, Sammy," Morgan teased, crossing his arms.

B.J. was suddenly glaring at Sammy. "You aren't supposed to say anything," he hissed in a low whisper that caused Sammy to grimace.

"Oh yeah, I forgot." He looked contrite, but then the words came flying out of him in a rush. "When a girl turns pink, it means she likes a boy. And when she drops stuff, too."

Morgan took in her hot cheeks, which she was certain were fire-engine red. "So I guess that means you better go tell Rowdy she likes him."

Both boys looked confused. Jolie was relieved—instead of being embarrassed, she found the scene touching. In their minds, the boys were just trying to help out the clueless adults.

"Morgan." B.J. spoke carefully as if explaining something to a two-year-old. "She likes *you*."

Sammy shoved him. "You weren't supposed to *say* it!"

B.J. glared at him. "*You* did and Morgan had it all mixed up!"

Rowdy sauntered over, bringing Ms. Jo and Mabel with him. Nana came from the other side of the room with the older boys trailing her. Jolie suddenly wanted to crawl into a hole.

"Did I hear my name? Morgan, what's up? You walk in and the kiddos start to fight?"

Ms. Jo didn't miss a beat. "You two looked like you just choked down a live cat for lunch. And I'm not talking about B.J. and Sammy. Jolie, why are you so pink?

If I didn't know any better, I'd think you're a little flustered."

She did not need this. She really, really didn't. Fighting a river was easier than this.

"Do you feel well?" Mabel chimed in. "Maybe you have a fever, honey. Maybe Morgan needs to take you home."

"Good idea," Nana chimed in. "Morgan, why don't you take poor Jolie home."

"Whoa!" Jolie boomed, stopping the chatter erupting around the room. She knew a hoodwink when she saw one. "There is *nothing* wrong with me. I certainly don't need to go home. Now, weren't Rowdy and Morgan invited here to taste-test these goodies? Because I'm in the mood for pie!"

It was one thing for her to be having thoughts about Morgan. It was altogether another thing for this entire room of folks knowing it!

Thankfully Mabel led the boys away to set up for the tasting. Only problem, that left her standing alone with Morgan. "That was awkward—talk about being on the hot seat," she said, forcing herself to look at him.

"Is that what that was? Felt more like a frying pan." He chuckled.

Jolie's traitorous thoughts went straight to thoughts of the kiss beside the river. His gaze dropped to her lips and she knew he was thinking about it, too.

"I'm sorry I haven't gotten back to you about us going back to the river," he said.

"We better get over there before they start up again." Jolie knew this was not the time or place to discuss what had happened between them.

Besides that, she wasn't sure at all what to say about that day…which was exactly why she'd been avoiding him. She'd been a disaster that day. It was embarrassing, and the fact that she'd been so distraught that she'd thrown herself into his arms and cried like a baby—that was the worst.

Chapter Fourteen

On Monday morning a few days after the pie fiasco, Jolie drove up to the schoolhouse to find the boys huddled in the front yard in deep conversation. The instant she stepped out of her Jeep, they busted apart, looking like guilty puppies that had just torn up her flower beds. Something was up.

"Hey, guys." She strode over to them as if she suspected nothing. "How are y'all today?"

"We're good." Wes grinned, excitement glistening in his pale green eyes. The teen looked more like a grown man than any of the kids, even Joseph, though he wasn't as tall. He was muscular and serious, unless he was thinking of an adventure. He was ready to finish school and get into college on the roping team. Life on the ranch had been good for him.

"How are you?" he asked her, stuffing his hands into his pockets. "You doing okay?"

She wasn't sure what to make of his line of questioning. Did she hear concern in his voice?

"Yeah, how are you?" Sammy asked as all the other boys chimed in.

"I'm fine, fellas. What's with all the worry?" She

looked at Wes and then Joseph for answers. "What's going on?"

Wes shifted his weight from one scuffed boot to the other. "Well, I, ah, I was surfing the Net last night looking at your YouTube videos," he added. "And well, we've looked at it before, all the amazing stuff you can do in a kayak. It's really cool seeing you coming down those rapids and over those sixty-foot falls. It blew me out of the water. You're awesome, Jolie. But, man…" His words trailed off…worry filled his eyes.

Dread filled Jolie.

"We came across your accident." Joseph was the one who said the words, his lips tight with concern. "We hadn't seen that. You almost *died,* Jolie." He raked his fingers through his too-long hair, reminding her of what Morgan did when he was upset. "It was bad."

Bad didn't begin to tell the story.

"It was," she said, trying to figure out what else to say but coming up empty.

"People were screaming on the video," Wes said, "going crazy when they thought you weren't coming up. Then your kayak came loose and it seemed like forever before you surfaced."

Jolie's stomach rolled. Inhaling slowly, she counted to ten, fighting hard to keep her nerves steady. Falling apart in front of the boys twice was unacceptable to her. She was stronger than that.

Please, God, hold me up. Take me past this moment when I'm unable to hold myself up.

She searched for words of assurance for the boys who were so concerned that most of them couldn't speak. Their care steadied her.

"What happened?" Sammy asked, touching her arm. "How did you live through that?"

"By God's grace, Sammy. By God's hand." It was true. "Only God could have given me the extra air it took to be under the water all that time. There are things in life that can only be explained by God's interventions, guys. And me surviving my accident was one of them."

"I don't see how you can get back in your kayak after that." Coming from Mr. Thrill Seeker himself, Wes's words startled her.

"In all honesty, guys, it's time for me to come clean with you. I *can't* get in my kayak. I came here to try and get my head on straight, but the thought of getting back in the water is rough. I'm trying, though. It's just taking some time."

"That's why you haven't been too keen on teaching us," Tony said.

"That's why."

"It's kinda like getting back on a bull," Wes said. "Only, a bull is more controllable than a river."

Jolie's nerves had calmed down a bit and she found Wes's words compelling. "Why do you say that?"

"Well, you can study a bull, know its habits and in some manner, predict his moves. A river, like the one you were on…" He hiked a shoulder, his brows crinkling skeptically. "You have no way of knowing what's beneath the surface. If that log hadn't come downstream from somewhere and lodged in that spot, then you'd have done your roll, come out of the water and finished that run. No preparation could have saved you from that log being there."

Jolie knew his words were true to some extent. Her training was similar to a bull rider preparing for the arena. However, there was always the element of surprise.

"I think that's the way it is in life, too. We have to

prepare and then give it to the Lord. That's what I did. I'm going to get over this and move forward, with God's help. And the time I'm spending here with you good-looking cowboys is helping me do that."

That won her some grins. Looking around at the group—at "her boys," as she'd begun to think of them—a lump formed in her throat and she ached with love of them. They were helping fill a spot that desperately needed filling in her soul.

"We like you being here," Sammy said, slipping his arm around her waist. "I'm glad you didn't die in that water."

She gave him a reassuring smile. "Me, too, because I'd have missed being here with you."

Sammy's expression was so full of hope that it stunned her. This child needed her.

The thought cut deep through Jolie. No one had ever needed her. Not like this. Yes, her team members needed her for her skills, and the points she could bring them. But the way Sammy needed her was different. He needed her for security, for support…for the love she could give him.

Thank You, God, for bringing me here.

She closed her eyes momentarily, the prayer filling her soul. Looking about the group, she realized that there were others who needed her, too.

Excitement surged through Jolie. She needed to talk to Morgan—to tell him what she was feeling. To share this new emotion with someone she cared for.

With the man she loved.

Morgan leaned back from his desk, weary from reading all the legalese that came with running the ranch. Taking in sixteen wards of the state did not come without an overabundance of paperwork. Keeping the ship running required staying on top of the forms that needed to be filled out. He'd taken on that part of the business when he'd signed on as partner with his dad.

Rubbing his eyes, Morgan was actually glad to have the office to hole up in for now. With Jolie being everywhere he was, it was hard to keep his head straight. Hard to keep his distance. Hard to stop thinking about kissing her.

That had been a gargantuan mistake on his part. Then, after the fiasco in the kitchen with the "spectators" watching their every move, he'd felt like even more of a fool than he had when he'd kissed her.

A man had to have a backbone.

Especially with an audience watching.

A knock on his door had him looking at the clock on the wall—nine-thirty. It had gotten late. "Come in," he called, expecting to see his dad, his brother or just about anyone other than Jolie.

So much for hiding out.

"Hi," she said, moving just inside the door. "Do you have a minute?"

Nope, all out of minutes. "Sure. I was just doing paperwork."

She glanced around his office, taking a few more steps into the room. "I like your space. It's you."

The walls had heavy, rich paneling. He had a cowhide rug on the floor, and Western art on the walls as well as pictures of boys with their animals at the county fair. Some of them holding championship banners and some were not. The projects weren't about the winning—they were about the experience of seeing something through. While Jolie's gaze had taken in the entirety of his office, it was the pictures of the kids that she had focused on.

"Thanks. I enjoy looking at those photos and seeing on their faces the satisfaction of a job well done."

Smiling, she perched on the edge of the leather chair across the desk from him. She wore jeans and a pale yellow blouse that caused her cinnamon hair to look darker and her emerald eyes to glow like jewels. They seemed less weary today, more alive. He hoped she was sleeping better.

He realized he was going to have to find some strength to handle being alone with her, or risk losing his pride.

"I thought we needed to talk. About several things. For starters, I need to apologize for falling to pieces down by the river. I—" She shook her head and closed her eyes briefly, drawing his attention to her long lashes against the warm golden skin of her cheeks. His gut clenched, remembering the soft feel of her skin.

"I'm not used to being so emotional. I'm sorry you had to pick up the pieces afterward."

"I should have kept my mouth shut and let you deal with your problem in your own time."

"No," she said. "I mean, you did the right thing making me try and face up to my fears. I'm glad I at least took a step toward the problem. Even though I ran away."

He cleared his throat. "I'm sorry I kissed you when you were…in a rough spot."

It's out there where it needs to be. Now move past it.

"About that. I'm sorry I threw myself at you."

That took him by surprise. The woman had been in a world of hurt. "I didn't see you do anything except need a little support. I was glad to give it."

Their gazes held as relief came over her face.

"Okay, then, we'll mark it up as 'I'm not sure what that was' and move on. Deal?" Her smile was warm.

"Deal."

"So, we need to discuss the boys."

The boys? "What's up?" he asked, trying to recover from the effect her smile had on him.

"The boys have been looking at videos of me competing. They finally came across the accident."

He should have known this would eventually happen. "What was their reaction?"

"Of course it scared some of them—all of them, actually. They wanted to know how I'm doing. I told them the truth—that I was having trouble. And they all understood. I told them I was trying to get my nerve back, that I'd come here to do that. Morgan, they were so sweet. I have to tell you that they've touched me deeper than I ever dreamed they could."

"They have a way of doing that." He took in his office for a moment. "That's why I'm here."

"I told them with God's help, I'd get back out there. I just wanted to tell you, and to thank you for trying to get me out there. I was a little miffed at you for pushing me. Maybe that was one of the reasons I got so...intense. I mean, when you're angry, it ups your emotions, so that could explain my anxiety."

"Were you mad at me the day you passed out?"

She frowned at him. "Okay, so maybe I'm just overly sensitive to the thought of getting in the water."

"That'd be my thought on the subject."

"Time will help. Anyway, I wanted to come and tell you what it means to me to be sharing time with the boys. Thanks for letting me be here."

What was he supposed to say to that? She was still leaving eventually, and they were still going to suffer because they'd all bonded to her. What did she expect that was going to do to them? "You're welcome." It was all he had.

Awkward silence filled the space between them. "Okay, then, I guess that's all I came to say." She stood to leave.

Say something.

Everything knotted in the pit of his stomach.

She headed toward the door. At last, impulse drove him out of his chair, skirting the desk in three strides. "Jolie—"

She'd spun at the same moment. "Yes?"

They stared at each other. Here they were *again*.

"I'm glad you came by. I've been swamped with paperwork that needs to be filed this week. So I've kind of been scarce."

She chuckled. "Well, that's a relief. I thought you'd been avoiding me."

"That, too," he admitted and smiled, loving her laugh. "Is there something else on your mind?"

"I'm thinking Sammy is better. We had a long talk today. That video gave me the opportunity to talk to all the boys, especially to Sammy, about how God is with us even in the bad times."

"Thank you for talking with him. Time will make everything better. Time and love."

Jolie's eyes brimmed with unshed tears. "Well, that is one thing the boys get here, that's for certain. Y'all are doing a great thing here, Morgan, and I'm proud to be a part of it. I've never been needed like I feel I am here. Today it hit me that I'm actually making a difference."

She got it. That dug deep into Morgan's soul. "Pretty cool feeling, isn't it?"

"It is. Well, I guess I better go and let you get back to work. Good night, Morgan."

"Good night, Jolie," he said. She was already heading out the door. He watched her cross the waiting area and push the door open. She didn't look back as she closed it behind her. The click of that door cracked like a gunshot in his head.

Jolie was falling for the boys and the boys had fallen for her. Raking his hand through his ruffled hair, he realized it was trembling.

So much for holding it together.

Jolie drove through the gate, headed toward her temporary home, her mind spinning in so many directions she wasn't sure what to think about first.

Morgan had looked tired but heartbreakingly handsome as always. She'd wanted to ask him more about his day, ask him how he'd been doing since he'd kissed her. Maybe kiss him again…

Nope, she was definitely not going to think about that. Pushing her hair out of her face, she was glad the top was rolled back on her Jeep—she needed as much fresh air clearing out her muddled brain as possible.

Her mind shifted to Sammy. She wanted to do more to make Sammy feel comfortable on the ranch; something that was special, and would involve the other boys, as well—something to give them all a sense of ownership in this ranch that was their home. What could it be?

She would seek the advice of Ms. Jo and Mabel. Nana, too.

Maybe she'd just ask the boys if they had any ideas about something they could do. Like maybe a festival. Maybe a reunion? Something they could enjoy…something that would keep them—and her—busy.

Something fun. Something different.

Something they could call their own.

Something that would let Morgan know she was serious about being here at Sunrise…serious about working with him.

Chapter Fifteen

When Jolie asked the boys the next day at school what kind of event they'd like to hold at the ranch, they took hardly a second to think about it. In fact, she was so startled by their quick response that she wasn't sure they'd understood what she was asking. But they had, and their answer was clear as day: they wanted to have a fishing tournament on the big lake.

"Wow, that was the quickest consensus I've ever seen among you fellas! Have y'all had fishing tournaments before?"

"Us older guys have." Wes grinned. "But it's been a while."

"We hear them talking about how fun it was all the time," Caleb interjected. "And Mr. Macintosh—you know Mr. Macintosh and Mr. Crump? Well, they have done some funny stuff."

"Yes, I know Mr. Macintosh and Mr. Crump. And I'm sure they do have some stories to tell," Jolie said, smiling as she thought of the town pot stirrers.

So it was decided that they were going to put on a fishing tournament and invite the town of Dew Drop to participate. The boys figured they'd charge a small fee and donate the money to the church's youth fund. Jolie thought this was an excellent idea—she was proud of the boys for wanting to donate to a good cause.

"What about you around the water?" Sammy asked.

She told him that they'd picked a good event, and it would be one more step toward getting her in the water. She didn't add that it wasn't the calm waters of the lake that shot her blood pressure sky-high—it was the raging sound of rapids.

By the end of the day Jolie had a plan and was pleased with how excited the boys were about the fishing tournament. They were even saying they could start having it every year. She liked that—loved it, in fact. It was exactly what she'd been after—an idea of their own that would tie them to the ranch in a special way.

Now she just had to run it by Morgan, but she was sure he would be all for it.

"Are you going to come work cattle with us?" Joseph asked, as they were all exiting the building. To her surprise, instead of racing off and claiming freedom, they lingered.

"I hadn't thought about it," she said. "I really need to see Morgan."

"Oh, then it's your lucky day—he's gonna be with us," Joseph drawled in his best Morgan imitation. "Come on. We're gonna vaccinate and tag 'em, and brand some, too."

Sammy grabbed her arm. "Come on with us. *Please*."

Jolie could do nothing other than agree when the boys took her arms and pulled her along to the barn. Saddling up her horse, she listened to the excited chatter filling the stables as all her boys saddled up, too. Jeans were a staple on the ranch and she wore them to work most days, so at least she was prepared for this spontaneous change of plans. Slipping her foot into the stirrup she boosted herself into the saddle. It creaked beneath her weight as she settled into it, and joy settled into her.

She was glad the boys had insisted she come.

Riding out of the barn with the guys, Sammy came up beside her on Cupcake, his control better than it had been. "Goodness, you're looking like a regular old grizzly cowpoke. Awesome job, little man."

He grinned proudly. "I don't even need any help anymore. Joseph or Wes or Mr. Pepper have to cinch the saddle up for me usually, but I got under there myself today."

Sammy's pride in his accomplishment put a smile on her face that was so big it nearly hurt. "You're a regular cowboy now, Sammy."

"I know, and who woulda thought it? I mean, I never even saw a horse except in pictures before I came here. And now I'm a cowboy."

Jolie laughed. The sun was bright in the indigo sky as it beat down on them. As beautiful as it was, it couldn't begin to compare to the joy that filled her watching Sammy snap his bootheels against his horse's belly, urging it into a trot to meet Wes and Joseph at the head of the gang.

Thank You.

The prayer of thanks eased out of her. And as she rode out with the boys, looking like a posse from an old Western, she conversed with the Lord all the way, thanking Him for the blessings in her life, for the renewing of her spirit, which she hadn't even realized needed renewing, and for the way He took bad situations and made them good.

One of God's many promises whispered through her mind. *I will never leave you or forsake you.* It was true.

By the time they made it to the corral where the cowboys were working a huge herd of cattle, she'd finished praying and moved on to a loud, excited conversation with the boys about all their plans for the fishing tournament.

Life was good.

The instant the men came into view, Morgan—unmistakable in the way he sat in his saddle, so erect and proud—broke from the herd and loped in their direction. His straw Stetson tugged low over his penetrating eyes, his face covered in a sheen of perspiration and dust, he looked rugged and powerful. He set Jolie's pulse galloping as he took his hat off, smiled a welcome at the boys and rode straight to her.

"This is a nice surprise." A gorgeous smile cut across his tanned face—a smile just for her, cutting deep into her heart.

"The boys hijacked me and wouldn't take no for an answer." She grinned back at him. Mercy, mercy, mercy, she was going to have to hug each and every one of them for it, too.

Life, Jolie realized as Morgan spun his horse and took up beside her, still grinning, wasn't just good—it didn't get any better.

It was a scorcher of a day, although September was racing by faster than a wild mustang charging for open pastures. Morgan knew it would start cooling down over the next few weeks, but for now, summer was stretching out and taking everything it could get.

Jolie didn't seem to mind the heat as she worked right alongside the boys and men. She'd been branding and tagging with Sammy, encouraging him the whole time. Watching her made his chest feel tight.

She looked up from where she had a knee on a calf, holding it so Sammy could brand it.

The faster summer went by, the sooner she'd be gone.

The sooner he'd be safe.

The sooner he'd miss her again.

The caustic scent of burning hair signaled that Sammy had been successful.

"Great job!" Jolie exclaimed the instant Sammy had done the deed and she let the calf up to jog away. Sammy had been worried about hurting the calf, and Jolie had explained that God had made cattle's hides thick for a reason. After that, the boy had had no problem wanting to learn the age-old trade of cattle country. Now, he was grinning from ear to ear.

"I did it!" he yelped, giving Jolie a high five. "You're one good cowgirl, Jolie. Let's get another one."

"Send out the signal and Wes will cut one from the group for us."

Sammy whipped off his hat and whooped and Wes nodded his way, lifted his rope and sent a loop flying through the air. He and Joseph were bringing in the calves while the younger boys helped the ranch hands minister brands and vaccines, ear tags and whatever else the calf needed. Jolie had jumped right in there, not minding the grime that went with the job.

She was a tough cookie with a soft interior—and he had a weakness for cookies.

Morgan struggled with wanting more from Jolie every moment he was awake, and even while he was asleep. After seeing her last night, he'd had a very restless night.

"You sure do look like a man in need of a little distraction," Rowdy said, drawing up beside him. Morgan hadn't even realized Rowdy was riding over from where he'd been overseeing the action on the far side of the corral.

"What's that supposed to mean?" he grunted, not happy that he'd been lost in thoughts about Jolie—and even more unhappy that he'd been caught.

Rowdy laughed. "Morg, you're in la-la land."

His eyes narrowed to slits. "The sun is in my eyes."

What a stupid thing to say, McDermott! It just made the goofy grin on Rowdy's face get goofier.

"So, you've got it bad again, haven't you?" he asked, turning serious.

"Last time I looked I felt fine. Didn't know I had anything."

"You know what I'm talking about." He thumped his heart with his fist. "Right here, looks like to me. I'm not sure how to react to it, either."

So his brother was a wise guy with eyes of a hawk. "Okay, so I'm a little messed up."

"A *little.* You better shore up those leaks in the dam if you don't want everyone who looks at you to know you're 'a little messed up.'"

Morgan rubbed his jaw, stubble stiff against his fingertips. "I've got my feelings cinched up tight, Rowdy. She's going to leave again—there is no doubt in my mind that she will, come December. And I'll be a big part of getting her ready to do that." Morgan took a moment to look at her before he went on. "I've been praying about this and I know that she's meant for bigger things. She's reaching a multitude of folks out there. Last night I saw a video of her at a children's hospital, encouraging kids who have stars in their eyes over her. A kid's mother took the video and posted it because Jolie went there without an entourage or a camera crew. She went because she wanted to. She's the real deal, Rowdy. Too much ability to be here wasting away on a ranch in the middle of Texas."

Rowdy shook his head. "Don't belittle what you do here on this ranch with these kids. You're not wasting away doing what you do, are you?"

"No," Morgan denied emphatically. "I love every minute of making sure the boys get what they need."

"Then why should it be any different for Jolie?"

"It's not the same. Here she'd have no spotlight and no chance to do the work she does, inspiring people. It's just not the same." And it wasn't.

Nope, come the end of this term, she'd be gone, and he'd have helped her get back out there where she belonged. It was time to head back to the river. And this time, she was getting in.

Chapter Sixteen

"It was awesome today!" Sammy gushed, pulling a feed bucket over to where the fellas were gathered at the back of the stables, covered in dirt, their faces streaked with sweat. He'd had more fun today than ever. And Jolie had hugged him and been so excited for him.

"Sammy's right, that was awesome. I *loved* it. But, so, what do y'all think?" Caleb asked, looking at Wes and Joseph.

"I seen what y'all been talkin' about," B.J. said, rocking on his bucket, his face still red as an apple from all their hard work. "Morgan, he was watching Jolie a bunch. Does that mean he loves her?"

Wes was chewing on a long piece of hay and he pulled it out of his mouth and grinned. "It's a start. I was watching him, too, and he's got it bad."

"Got what bad?" Sammy asked. "Love?"

He pointed at Sammy with his hay. "I think so, my man. I think so. Don't you, Joseph?"

"I hope so. We've been trying hard to get them together on the quiet, and they seem to like each other most of the time. But I'm not sure about all the time. That worries me."

Tony hung his leg over the rung of the stall. "Then we just got to try harder. Keep it up, man. In them romances, love takes time. Morgan don't look at anyone else like he looks at Jolie. Don't forget the day by the truck after the volcano. They were seriously thinking about kissing. You all know it."

"And Jolie was all pink in the kitchen," Sammy reminded them. "Remember?"

"Love's about more than just wanting to kiss or turning pink," Joseph said. "But I agree with Wes—let's keep finding ways to get them together. This fishing tournament is going to fit right in. Can y'all keep on keepin' this a secret? Everyone raise their hand who thinks we should keep trying to help Jolie and Morgan fall in love."

Everybody raised their hand, and Sammy and B.J. grinned at each other.

"Good," B.J. said. "'Cause I want Jolie to be my mom. Even if she is scared of the water. I don't care about that. I can still love her just as good. You can, too, right, Sammy?"

Sammy nodded, his insides feeling all funny thinking about it. He knew he could love Jolie, but he wasn't real sure she—or anyone—could ever really love him. If his parents didn't stick around… He stopped himself. His parents would come back—they would. But until then, it would be nice to have Jolie and Morgan be his ranch parents.

"Yeah, B.J., I can love her, too," Sammy finally said.

Two weeks after they'd come up with the idea of the fishing tournament, Jolie headed to the newspaper office in town with the official advertisement in hand.

Since they'd first thought of the idea, the tournament had morphed into a really big day—it wasn't just about fishing anymore. There were going to be all sorts of competitions and events. And the boys also wanted to add a little arena fun for the kids who didn't want to fish.

They'd decided to have the tournament the week before Thanksgiving, which didn't give them long with the weeks flying like they were.

As she pulled up in front of the newspaper building, Chili and Drewbaker were sitting on the church pew outside.

"Stupendous idea about the fishin' tournament, Jolie. Folks are talkin', excitement is abuildin'," Chili commented as she closed her door and stepped up onto the sidewalk.

"That's the truth." Drewbaker sliced off a sliver of soft wood from the elaborate bird he was carving. "I even heard we're having a competition on who's got the most decorated boat. Whoever thought about decorating a boat?"

"Well," Jolie chuckled, "that came from Nana, actually. She thought it would add a little something to the pot to have a bit more competition. She thought she'd put you fellas on the spot with decorating."

"Sounds like something she'd do." He scratched his chin with the knuckles of his hand, holding his knife. "I bet ol' Jo and Mabel are gonna have a doozied-up dingy."

"Don't you know it," Chili grumbled. "I 'spect they're already patting themselves on the back in congratulations on winning that part of the tournament."

Jolie saw the competitive wheels turning behind the two men's watchful eyes. "Well, you know them, I'm sure they have big plans."

Drewbaker squinted, drawing his bushy brows together, his face the picture of a man who loved a good contest. "I hear there's a paddle rule. No motors. I'm thinking y'all need to renege on this no-motor policy. Maybe give the teams whose ages add up together to be more than, say, a hundred and twenty-five, the opportunity to use a trolling motor."

Jolie laughed. "Boy, you've got this all figured out, don't you?"

That won her a hoot from Chili. "When two old codgers like us are fighting for our lives with the young studs you've got out there on the ranch, then you betcha we're getting things figured out. This takes strategy."

"And I can tell you're good at that."

Two wide, mischievous smiles spread across their faces. Jolie loved that everyone was having a good time with this, and she was thrilled that folks wanted to help out the kids. Many ranches around had offered the use of their boats because they knew that the ranch wouldn't have enough for all the boys to be on the water at the same time.

Morgan had teamed the boys up so that those with less experience had someone more experienced in the boat with them. Morgan himself was competing with Sammy and Jolie was very thankful for that.

Wes and Joseph had been disappointed that they hadn't gotten to team up together, but they made her proud by being good sports about helping out the younger fellas. Plus now they had their own competition going—Jolie was holding her breath to see which of the two would bring in the largest bass.

"Don't you be giving away any secret tips to the likes of them," Ms. Jo hollered from across the street. She'd come outside and was glaring their way with her fist on her hip.

"I'm not, I promise," Jolie called.

"Hey, you just stay over there and let the woman talk

to us all she wants about this," Drewbaker returned. "Y'all are goin' down."

Chili hooted again. "Like a lead tank."

Jolie shook her head. "Boys, you do know Mabel and Ms. Jo fish together out at Patrick Lake all the time. They even have an alligator they've named."

"We know. That don't mean we're scared of them."

"Surely don't, Drewbaker," Chili agreed. "It surely don't."

Jolie excused herself before she got into any more trouble, and made her way to the newspaper office to drop off the ad. A little while later she was headed back home with plans to work out. She nearly drove her Jeep into the ditch when she saw Morgan's truck parked in her driveway with him leaning against the tailgate, boots crossed at the ankles and a long strand of grass sticking from between his teeth as he waited with arms crossed. Her pulse skittered to life as if it had been dead to the world until right now.

"Well, hey, there, mister," she said, hopping from her Jeep. "You sure are lookin' lazy all propped up by the tailgate."

A slow smile eased its way from one corner of his lips to the other beneath the shade of his hat.

Her toes curled and her stomach tilted.

"If you think I need something to occupy my time, then you need to give me something to do," he drawled.

"Hold on to your hat, bucko, or I just might do that." Not in any of the ways that were flying through her mind, of course. No hugging or kissing the cowboy. Nope, none of that.

"Sounds like a plan. Or if you don't have one, I'll tell you what mine is."

"I'd be willing to hear yours," she said, slamming

the door. She strode to lean against the tailgate beside him, forcing herself to be at ease. His husky chuckle did nothing to help settle her butterflies.

"I'm here to see if you'd like to go down to the river for a rematch."

She gave him a grimace. "Talk about messing up a perfectly good afternoon."

He leaned so that his shoulder was pressing against hers. "I come in peace. You realize it's been nearly a month since we tried this? You're sleeping better, I think."

"That's true. Not always, but for the most part I am. The nightmares are only a few times a week now instead of a few times a night."

"So don't you think it's time to push yourself some more?"

Jolie took in some air—it was time to tell Morgan about the decision she'd made. "Morgan, maybe we should talk."

He shifted to face her, still leaning against the tailgate. In the past few weeks they'd worked together to get the fishing tournament in order and they'd relaxed around each other somewhat. Jolie was certain that Morgan felt the anchor load of attraction that she felt, and had always felt. And yet they'd never mentioned the kiss they'd shared on the banks of the river again, not since the night in his office.

She thought that was probably the way he wanted it.

There was still a no-trespassing sign on his heart, and she was trying her hardest to mind the sign. But she knew it was useless. Her heart belonged to Morgan McDermott, even though she'd trampled his years ago. What Ms. Jo, Mabel and Nana said was true—Morgan had never been the same after her. It hurt knowing what she'd done to him.

She was praying that time would heal the wound between them. God could handle this, even if she couldn't.

"I decided last week that I'm retiring from competition."

Morgan looked like she'd hit him with a soggy fish, he looked so shocked. "That's a mistake and you know it, Jolie. I've told you before you would regret doing something rash like that. You'll always know you let fear have its way with you. What kind of example is that?"

His words were what she'd expected, to a degree. "I didn't say I wasn't getting back in the water. But I don't want to compete anymore." She took a deep breath, preparing herself to reveal the next part of her decision to him. "I want to be here on the ranch. I'd like an extended contract."

"No."

For a moment, Jolie wasn't sure she'd heard him correctly.

"Haven't you been pleased with what I've been doing?" she asked.

He looked torn for a moment and she felt her heart sink. She'd been working her hardest, trying to do a great job because the boys deserved it. She'd also wanted to prove to Morgan she could do it. She'd been hoping for a firm "You've been doing a great job, Jolie," but that was most definitely not what she was getting.

"Well, that was eye-opening," she said. "Not sure what you expect out of your teachers, but when a girl gives it her whole heart and that's not good enough, that's pretty rough. Especially when I know I've been doing a knock-out job—the boys' grades and their attitudes reflect that."

"There is no denying you've done an excellent job. But this is about you, Jolie. I won't be a part of your not doing what you need to do."

"Excuse me, you don't know what I need to do and what I don't need to do."

"That so?"

"That's so." They'd moved within inches of each other, which is what always happened when they argued. How it happened was beyond Jolie, but it always did.

He searched her eyes. "I know you," he said, his breath warm against her skin, sending a shiver racing down her spine.

She shook her head, both to clear it and to deny what he was saying. "Not so. Or you'd know being here with these boys means the world to me. Being here…with *you.*" There—she'd said the truth. It was barely audible, but she'd said it. "It means the world to me, Morgan."

He lifted his hand and it hovered for a moment, then gently touched her hair. Like a featherlight kiss, his gaze rested on her lips, making her step toward him.

"No." The word flew from him as he stepped back, breaking the pull between them. "I won't let you do this. You love what you do. You're afraid to admit it, though, and I won't let you use me and this ranch as a crutch."

"I *love* you, Morgan." It was true—she'd never stopped loving him. She was certain that what she felt for him now was the love of a grown woman who knew her own mind. "Coming back here and being near you, seeing the man you've become, watching you with the boys and witnessing the dedication that you have to them and this ranch, it just makes my heart ache with regret that I wasn't here to help build this with you."

Her heart felt swollen inside her chest.

Morgan's eyes flashed. "This would never work,

Jolie." Grabbing his hat, he tore it from his head and slapped his thigh. "This will not work," he said again, and in one swift motion he pulled her into his arms and covered her mouth with his, stealing her breath. Jolie could feel the years of loss in his kiss, in the iron clasp of his embrace as he crushed her to him. And she returned his kiss with all the regret of lost years and the joy of homecoming. She trembled in his arms and was glad to have them for support. Her heart thundered in time with his and when he suddenly broke free and backed off, it felt as if a part of her had been ripped away.

He glared at her, swallowing hard as if there was a boulder lodged in his throat, his chest rising and falling. "I watched you leave once and had to pick up my heart." His voice was gruff. "I tried to be fine with it. Even thought I was in love with Celia. But she called me on it the night before we were to marry. Did you know that? She didn't marry me because she realized I was still in love with you."

She shook her head. "I knew the wedding had been called off, but I didn't know why. I'm not sure anyone did."

Are you still in love with me now? she wanted to ask, only the words wouldn't come. His glare held them off like a shield.

"She was right. But Jolie, I picked up my life and I've moved on. I was happy finally. And then you came back." He shook his head again, and bent and picked up his hat from the ground where it had fallen, forgotten in the midst of their embrace.

"I won't be renewing your contract, Jolie. You need to get back to the life you love. I'll help you all I can, but I can't do this—I can't go backward."

She couldn't breathe, couldn't speak as she watched

him stalk to his truck and slam the door behind him. He was already halfway out of the driveway before she could move.

Numb, she walked to the porch and sank to the step, too dazed to do anything else.

Chapter Seventeen

He'd really done it this time. He had completely lost his mind.

Yes, sir, no doubt about it, he was a raving lunatic. Why else would he have been fool enough to kiss Jolie after she fired a bombshell right at his heart?

Crazy—therein lay the problem.

Crazy *and* a fool.

Now he knew what had been wrong all along. There was obviously something in his brain that was broken when it came to Jolie.

He didn't like it one bit.

But he didn't have a clue how to fix it.

Gravel spewed behind him as he drove like the lunatic that he was down the road leading to his house. He'd built the place with his bare hands the year after Jolie left. He'd put a lot of sweat—and yes, tears—into the house. It had been a refuge away from the eyes of everyone in Dew Drop. Driving into the yard, he was relieved when he saw the stone-and-log fortress—home. It was sturdy. It had clean lines and hard edges. Just like his heart.

His grandmother kept telling him it needed a woman's touch to soften it up—some flowers, and a couple of trellises of roses and morning glories.

It was fine like it was, he'd told her.

He walked in through the heavy door that he'd made himself from the oaks in his woods, with hand-sanded planks and bold, strong hinges that were meant to last a lifetime. Strong, dependable, reliable.

Slamming the door behind him, Morgan's steps echoed as he walked straight through the empty house and out the back door onto the deck that overlooked the river.

Had he built this house to keep her memories at bay? Or had he built this house on the crook of the river to remind him of her?

The question slammed into him the minute the sound of the flowing water reached him.

Grasping the deck railing, he glared down at the river twenty feet away. His life had been in order. It had been settled.

And now this.

I love you.... Her words reverberated through his thick skull. *Coming back here and being near you, seeing the man you've become, watching you with the boys and witnessing the dedication that you have to them and this ranch, it just makes my heart ache with regret that I wasn't here to help build this with you.*

Regret. He knew a thing or two about regret. He closed his eyes and prayed for God to throw him a lifeline.

Part of him clamored to go back and tell Jolie he wanted her here. However, he'd learned that love was about letting them go. It was about helping Jolie do what she was meant to do.

He wasn't giving in to any weakness this go-around.

Because if he gave in, if he opened his heart again and then she left, he knew the pain would be worse than the first time.

No. Girding up the door was the best thing.

But the kiss. His pulse kicked up like a buckin' bronc just thinking about that kiss. How was he ever supposed to forget it? He couldn't and he knew it.

When she left…at least he'd have the memory. But it was going to take everything he had to stay strong and let her go.

Jolie went through the week—which was blessedly busy—on remote much of the time, but to her surprise, she was able to enjoy the boys' excitement in getting ready for Saturday's fun.

Focus, Jolie, she kept telling herself. *Focus on the fishing tournament, on keeping sixteen boys in line, on putting Morgan's rejection on the back burner.*

The boys weren't the only ones who were excited. Nana, Ms. Jo and Mabel had prepared all manner of goodies for the occasion with help from Edwina, T-Bone and many others from town. No one would starve come Saturday—that was for certain.

Dew Drop and the surrounding area had been invited and a huge number of folks were going to turn out. Thirty-two teams had applied for the tournament, which was a great number—not too many and not too few. The boys had been figuring out how to decorate their boats and for the most part, they had kept it simple, not wanting to distract themselves from the main goal, which was to hook the biggest fish.

Many of the boats had forgone the decorations completely, because it had been optional, but some were done up in style. There were boats with umbrellas, including one that had an inflatable palm tree sitting next to the trolling motor, which, of course, would remain off because they had to use paddles. Another had an American flag flying. Sammy and Morgan had mounted a set of sun-bleached cow horns on the front of their boat and Sammy was proud of it. She'd laughingly offered to put a big red bow on the horns for added decoration. Horrified, they'd declined her offer.

Morgan had been around some, keeping busy with the boys and keeping interaction with her to a minimum. She was fine with that. She still wasn't clearheaded about what had happened between them. She'd told Morgan she loved him, and he hadn't said it back. They'd shared the kiss of a lifetime and she'd felt certain his whole heart had been in that kiss, and yet instead of telling her he loved her, he'd refused to let her stay. This really confused her, and by the end of the week it was becoming increasingly hard to focus. Best bet was to do as they were doing and let it steep—for now.

But it was not a foregone conclusion that they were done. Oh no, not by a long shot.

Saturday dawned, cooling off at eighty-five degrees—perfect for Texas in November. As up-and-down as the weather was in the fall months, it could easily have dawned at sixty degrees and wet. God had given them a beautiful day, though, and for that Jolie was thankful.

The lake area was beautiful, too—a steep hill sloping down to a picturesque lake surrounded by large oak and cedar trees. Upon Jolie's arrival, a group of deer lifted their heads from eating acorns beneath the oaks and raced for cover within the nearest stand of trees. She took a moment to enjoy watching them before driving the rest of the way down to the dock.

It wasn't long before things started rolling. The boys'

boats had been carried down the night before and sat ready to slide into the lake, palm trees, cow horns, flags and umbrellas included.

Rowdy, Tucker, Randolph and most of the cowboys who worked on the ranch showed up to help direct people and offer assistance where needed. They were also in charge of the arena event, which the boys had decided was going to be a cow-dressing competition. Jolie could only imagine the fun the kids were going to have treating cattle like Barbie dolls.

Nana and Ms. Jo were unpacking a truckload of goodies and Mabel was setting up the drink station, with the help of several of their friends from church. Jolie realized early into this fundraiser that the folks of Dew Drop were just as generous with their time and money as they'd ever been. A feeling of peace filled her—it was nice to belong here.

She only wished Morgan felt it was nice for her to belong here, too.

"Where in the world are those two loudmouth whittlers?" Ms. Jo asked about thirty minutes before it was time for the boaters to put in. The grounds were crowded with folks milling around and kids running and playing. Everything was set—everything except Chili and Drewbaker. They hadn't shown up yet.

"I don't know. This isn't like them, is it?" Jolie asked, checking her watch one more time.

"Not on your life. Those two are usually first responders when it comes to being on time."

Ms. Jo's words were barely out of her mouth when a honking horn drew everyone's attention. Drewbaker's dusty blue, sixty-something Ford pickup topped the hill, heading slowly down the big slope toward everyone. Both men were grinning as everyone gaped at what they were pulling on the flatbed trailer behind the truck.

It was a round metal watering trough, about six feet across. It had two folding chairs sitting in it with a cooler in the center. On the edges they'd mounted fishing pole holders, and several poles stood at attention.

"Heavens to Betsy, what is *that?*" Ms. Jo snapped, marching to meet them as they eased to a halt.

"Here we are, secret weapon in tow," Drewbaker said jauntily as he climbed from his old truck with a grin.

Chili's cheeks were pink with excitement and cheer as he hurried around the front of the truck to where a crowd had gathered, studying their contraption. "Ain't she a beaut?" he bragged.

"She's a beaut, all right," Ms. Jo snorted. "Secret weapon—ha! I'll have to see it to believe it."

"Does it float?" Wes asked, sauntering up, eyeing the contraption with interest.

Drewbaker's mouth dropped open. "Does a dog wag its tail? Sure it floats!"

"But will it tip over?" Joseph asked skeptically.

"Well, now, there's an interesting possibility," Chili chuckled. "Me and ol' Drewbaker might just be takin' ourselves a little bath if it tips one way or the other." He tugged out two life vests and held them up. "Just in case."

Morgan stepped through the crowd, brushing past Jolie as he went. The woodsy scent of his cologne teased her senses. *Unfair,* she thought.

"Fellas, I'm not sure what to make of this, but I have to say I'm interested in seeing what happens when y'all climb in it."

"How do you get it in the water?" Caleb asked.

"Yeah," called a few people in the crowd.

Good question. Because the trough wasn't on a regular boat trailer and there was no curve to the bottom, she assumed they would have to get the boys to carry it down to the water.

"If we could get a little assistance," Drewbaker said. Climbing up on the flatbed trailer, he began gathering the fishing poles from their holders. He handed some to Sammy and Caleb and B.J., who had raced to help.

Drewbaker then lifted the fold-up chairs out and handed them off to a couple of boys, and the ice chest, too. When the boat thing was empty, he had Morgan, Tucker and Rowdy help him and Chili lift it to the ground, then tip it on its side and simply roll it down the hill to the end of the dock. Once there, they turned it upright and eased it into the water.

"Well, I'll be," Jolie murmured.

Chili used a rope tied to the handle to secure it to the dock. Now all that was left was their managing to get in the thing.

Ms. Jo and Mabel watched with squinted eyes.

"I have to give it to the old codgers, it's original." Mabel chuckled, shaking her head.

"They'll probably drown themselves before the day is done," Ms. Jo retorted. "Come on, Mabel, let's go show these fellas how it's done."

And so the day began.

The tournament was officially started with the wave of a flag, and everyone jumped into their boats and pushed out into the water ready for battle. Everyone, that is, except Drewbaker and Chili. They eased into their circular contraption very carefully, keeping their weight evenly distributed, grinning the whole time. Once in their seats they pushed off from the dock.

Drewbaker gave a salute, and to the amazement of

everyone watching, they floated out onto the lake like a dream!

Nana paused beside her. "I don't know about you, but I have a feeling the boys will vote that funny dinghy the winner."

Jolie chuckled. "If those two get dunked in the lake, it's a sure winner."

Nana's eyes widened. "I wouldn't put it past those two to do something like that on purpose if they aren't having any bites today."

A sudden squeal from the lake had them both zeroing in on Sammy and Morgan.

"I got one! I got one!" Sammy called. Morgan was sitting beside him in the small two-man boat, calmly showing him how to reel in the fish. Once he got it reeled in, he waved his pole in the air, the small fish dangling above their heads until Morgan grabbed it and took the hook from its mouth.

"That's good for both of them." Nana tilted her head to the side. "Morgan has been preoccupied and fairly irritable this week—more so than anytime since you got here. You wouldn't know anything about that, would you?"

Not wanting to discuss their situation even with Nana, Jolie hesitated. "Let's just say I might know something about it, and I don't know how to fix it."

Nana gave her a sympathetic smile. "This is what I was afraid of. I remember the first year after you left. I couldn't help Morgan with the pain, and I had to watch him work through it in his own way. 'He heals the brokenhearted and binds up their wounds'—I clung to that verse for Morgan, Rowdy and Tucker after their momma died. And I did it again for Morgan after you left. I knew he didn't love Celia." She shrugged. "I couldn't tell him that, though. Thankfully the poor girl had the gumption to realize it herself and do something about it." Her kind eyes looked steadily into Jolie's, and Jolie couldn't speak. "This can't be easy for either of you. I've been praying God's will—and you know He does have one. Even if we don't understand it. God's got a plan, Jolie."

Patting her on the arm, Nana headed toward the goody table. Jolie took a deep breath and studied Morgan from a distance. Sammy was keeping him busy, fidgeting on the boat seat and hooking his shirt almost every time he tried to cast his line. Morgan patiently worked with him.

Dear Lord, what is Your plan for my life?

"Please tell me," she whispered in the slight breeze. It was the first time that Jolie could remember actually asking God that question.

Morgan was trying hard not to laugh as Chili and Drewbaker were having a terrible time with a leak in their tub.

"They're biting better on your side," Chili said, poking his buddy in the shoulder with the tip of his pole. "And it's time for you to bail water and me to fish."

"Hang on to your horses. I think I have a bite," Drewbaker grumbled, keeping his fishing pole steady over the water.

Morgan and Sammy had been hearing bits of the fellas' conversation off and on all morning. It was entertaining, that was for sure. Fishing was normally a quiet sport, but not today on this lake. When a kid caught a fish, he whooped and his boat rocked with excitement—Morgan was glad he'd insisted on life vests. When a grown man caught a fish bigger than his neighbors', he whooped, too, and taunted them with his catch.

"I sure am liking this fishing," Sammy said, grinning when he pulled in his third bass of the morning. Holding it up proudly, Morgan chuckled.

"That's because you're whipping the pants off me."

Sammy shrugged. "I got the moves."

"Yeah, I guess you do."

"Hold on to your hat, Chili, I've got a bite! A big-un, too," Drewbaker yelped excitedly, drawing everyone's attention. His line stretched out and he began reeling in his catch. It was a fighter and the bass did a flip out of the water.

"Whoa, Nellie! That's a big-un," Chili said, halting his dipping. He shot to his feet in excitement, making the tub rock with force. It would have been fine except Drewbaker's chair tilted when Chili slammed back down in his seat. Hanging on to his pole, Drewbaker rode his chair as it slid with the rocking tub. To Morgan's surprise the tub stayed afloat as Drewbaker managed to get his good-size bass into the tub without bashing his buddy.

"I thought for sure they were goners," Sammy said, laughing.

Morgan was thoroughly enjoying fishing with the boy. Sammy was doing well in general, and seemed more settled now. The fact that he hadn't freaked out over the thought of the tub tossing the two whittlers into the lake was a good sign, too.

"Catch him," Drewbaker demanded, drawing their attention again. Chili was bent over, grasping at the bottom of the boat. "What's going on now?" Morgan called to the duo.

"The fish got loose in the bottom of the boat!" Chili yelled.

Drewbaker looked up, over the edge. "There's so

much water, he's swimmin' and thinkin' he's found a new home. We can't catch him!"

"You two need to just take that contraption to the shore right now," Ms. Jo demanded. "Serious-minded fisherwomen can't even think straight for all y'alls lollygagging and jammer-jawin'!"

Sammy grinned at Morgan, his big eyes bright. "This is the most fun I've had since I got here. I sure am glad I'm with you."

If that didn't get to a man, Morgan didn't know what would. "Kiddo, it's the most fun I've had in a long time, too."

It wasn't lost on him that all of this had been Jolie's idea. She was a good teacher, with an eye for making things special for the boys. He had to admit it—she would be a blessing to the program if she were to stay.

The question was, could he handle it if she did?

Chapter Eighteen

The fishing tournament was a success. The boys could not stop smiling and teasing each other after they got back on dry land. And they were thrilled with the results of the boat-decoration contest—it was no surprise when Jolie counted the votes from the jar and announced that the galvanized tub had won unanimously.

Jolie loved seeing everyone have a good time. Kids were running around playing kickball, and people were visiting and catching up while Morgan and his men unloaded the young cows for the cow-dressing contest. She felt a rush of pride that her boys had made this day happen, with a little help from her. And from Morgan.

She and Morgan made a good team.

Pushing the thought from her mind, she went over to help organize the kids into six different groups—there were about seventy in all, in a vast range of ages. After they were organized, she lined them up around the temporary arena Morgan had hauled in for the occasion. She put Sammy in a group with Wes and several kids who were his age and younger—she hoped he would feel like the leader of the younger ones.

"Jolie, can you help?" Rowdy called to her. Climbing through the portable railed panels of the temporary corral, she crossed to where the cowboys were gathered around Morgan. His gaze landed on her and he lifted his chin in greeting.

"Your job is to pick a cow, stay by her and help out if needed. The object of the game is for the kids to dress the cow using the clothing they have on. Your job is to make sure no one takes off anything they shouldn't."

"Seriously?" Jolie asked. This was a new event for her.

Rowdy chuckled. "You'd be surprised just how inventive kids can be during a cow dressing."

"I hope we don't end up with a bunch of streakers running around."

"It will be fine," Morgan assured her, speaking directly to her for the first time that day. They had spoken a few times during the week, but their conversations had been quick and strictly about business. His eyes were distant, the wall between them firmly in place. Jolie looked away, not wanting him to see how much this hurt her.

"Okay, take your places. Two men to an animal," Morgan said. Cowboys scattered instantly.

Jolie didn't move quickly enough and to her dismay ended up beside Morgan and his cow.

Of all the luck.

Looking about as happy as she was about their situation, he continued giving instructions through a megaphone. "Okay. Here we go. Dress your cow."

Like a flood of ants attacking a bowl of sugar, the kids came over the railings of the arena and headed straight for the cows. The teams had to wrestle the cow to the ground, then dress it. Laughter and hooting erupted as the clothes went flying—kids stuffed colored socks on cows' hooves, stripped off long-sleeved shirts and tried to pull them over the cows' front legs and wrapped shirts around the animals' necks. By the time Morgan blew his whistle, the animals were running around with clothing flopping everywhere.

Everyone was laughing hard by the time it was over, and kids were jumping up and down with excitement. When Jolie met Morgan's eyes, she knew he was thinking the same thing she was: they'd done a good thing.

And for today, she was satisfied with that.

"Good job, Jolie." Morgan tipped his hat at her.

"Thanks. I was glad to do it." She pinned him with a steady look. "We make a good team."

Before Morgan could say anything else, Jolie turned and headed for the goody table. She needed some chocolate chip cookies to keep her mouth busy—the last thing she wanted to do right now was say too much.

With any luck, Morgan McDermott would spend some quality time thinking on what she'd just said.

When Jolie returned home from three days in Houston for Thanksgiving—where she'd been forced to answer endless questions from her parents about being on the ranch with Morgan—she headed straight for Randolph's office. She'd loved her visit with her family, but she'd missed the kids and she'd missed Morgan so much it hurt.

Driving up to the office, she was relieved to see that Morgan's truck wasn't there.

She entered the small lobby. Randolph's door was open and she rapped gently on the door frame to get his attention.

"Jolie," Randolph said, standing and waving her inside.

"I know I've done a good job," she said after explaining why she'd come.

Randolph, who looked so much like an older Morgan, leaned back in his chair. "You've done a fantastic job, Jolie, but Morgan is a partner in the ranch. He has a say in who will teach the boys on a full-time basis. If Morgan isn't on board, I can't give you the contract. I'm very sorry about that."

She'd known what he'd say, but she had to at least ask. In her heart of hearts she knew this was where she belonged. She'd been praying, and listening for God's will, and she had to see if He would open a door through Randolph.

Forcing down her disappointment, she rose. "Thank you for everything. I understand." Turning, she headed for the door.

"Jolie," Randolph called, his deep voice stopping her. "'Many are the plans in a man's heart. But it is the Lord's purpose that prevails.' That's Nana's favorite proverb."

"Yes, I've heard her quote it before."

"God's will is at work in your life. Remember that."

The words hit deep. "I will." She left, offering him a smile on her way out that probably looked as sad as it felt.

She hoped God let her in on the plan soon. Because she felt as if her life was here, on the ranch with the boys, and with Morgan. Without it, she had no idea who she was or what she was supposed to do.

Or how she was supposed to handle letting go of Morgan a second time.

"Something is wrong with Jolie," Wes said, looking at the group assembled around him behind the stables. He'd called the meeting because it was time to do something.

"Yeah, she's been quiet and real distracted this week." Joseph had his boot propped on the corral rung and was tapping his fingers on his knee. "I think she's worried about not being able to get in the water."

"Yeah," Wes agreed. "I heard her talking to someone about an advertisement she's supposed to shoot over the Christmas holidays. And she didn't look too happy when she got off the phone. It sounded like she's got her back up against the wall."

"She doesn't have to do it if she don't want to, does she?" Sammy asked.

"She's a professional kayaker," Wes stated. "She gets paid to do these ads. Her job is on the line, I think."

"But what about her being our teacher? And our ranch mom, like y'all told me?" B.J. asked.

The guys all looked at each other with uncertainty.

"Look—" Joseph pulled his boot off the rung and stood straight "—we want Jolie to stay, but she's got priorities. She's got to get past this bad thing that happened in her life. It's kind of how we've had to do it a little bit. I mean, we've each had some bad stuff—we know how hard it is to get past it."

Sammy looked sad. "Will she come back to us if she gets back in the water?"

"I don't know, Sammy," Joseph said.

He and Wes stared at each other for a long moment. Wes knew Joseph hated the look on the little kid's face as much as he did. And the other boys', too. They had to do something and they both knew it.

"Sometimes a person doesn't know what's in front of them till they face their fears."

"How do you know that, Joseph?" Sammy asked.

"I don't know. I heard it in a movie. It sounds right, though. I'm thinking Jolie and Morgan have this thing going on. Y'all have seen how they've been lookin' at each other lately."

"Kinda mad," B.J. said.

"And sad," Sammy added with a sigh. "When one isn't looking and they don't know we're watching."

"Yeah," everyone agreed at once.

"Couldn't Jolie teach us and still compete in kayaking?" Tony piped in.

"Maybe." Wes thought hard. "I'm just not sure."

Panic lit Sammy's face. "I don't want her to go."

"None of us do," Joseph said.

"Isn't there something we can do?" Caleb asked.

"Yeah." Tony stepped up. "We have to do something."

"We can pray that she stays," Joseph replied, perking up.

Sammy looked down at the dirt. "If we're good, maybe she'll stay."

Wes raked his hands through his hair, his heart hurting bad. He knew prayers didn't work. He'd prayed hard for his family not to fall apart, but God didn't always listen to prayers. He knew he couldn't tell the little kids that, though. They'd already been through enough, and it wasn't easy being a bunch of misfits that nobody wanted.

"Hey, you guys start praying. Me and Joseph will come up with something. Meanwhile, fellas, keep your ears and your eyes open. Anything you see or hear that could help us with a plan to get those two together, you tell us. If we get them to fall in love, then I betcha Jolie will stay."

Joseph and Wes looked at each other over the little kids' heads as they began to pray, hoping against hope that Wes was right.

Chapter Nineteen

A cold wind blew in from the north right after Thanksgiving. It matched the chill in Jolie's heart.

Blinking in the wind, she urged her horse to pick up speed as she rode across the open range. She needed the feel of the wind in her hair and the thunder of hooves beneath her. She hadn't been to the river's bend since she'd gotten back, and she had to go, even if she didn't want to.

Too many memories were there. It was where Morgan had asked her to marry him. It was where she'd said yes. It was there, on the banks of the river, that they'd fallen in love.

Today, feeling lost and confused, her time on the ranch almost up, she'd suddenly thought that if God was going to give her answers, maybe she would be able to hear Him at the river's bend. Or at least maybe she would be able to think clearly.

Nearing the curve in the gravel road leading to the river, she slowed her horse and rounded the corner at a slow trot.

Her heart stopped at what she saw. A log-and-stone house sat where she'd once dreamed of a having a home—and Morgan's truck was parked in the drive.

He'd never said a word.

Heart thudding, she slowly climbed from the saddle, tied up her horse and walked to the front door. It was beautiful, and looked hand-crafted. She ran her fingertips across the smooth surface, then, taking a fortifying breath, she knocked. Her heart pounded and her head was spinning with questions.

She'd never thought to ask where he lived. She'd never dreamed…

When there was no answer, she found herself walking around the beautiful house to the back—she had to see what it looked like. She halted when she saw the deck. It was exactly as she'd dreamed when she was seventeen—built on the edge of the steep hill with a beautiful view of the river below, and the setting sun. Morgan stood with his back to her, his elbows resting on the deck railing, a mug cupped between his hands.

Walking up the steps, she stopped on the last one.

"Morgan," she said, barely audible over the gentle sound of the river. It struck her then that she hadn't hyperventilated or freaked being close to the water. It had been part of her plan, coming here, hoping this would be the place she could make peace with her past—all of it. But she hadn't planned on finding this.

At the sound of his name Morgan straightened and swung around. "Jolie."

He took her breath away. He was the only man who'd ever made her feel the way she felt now, and the most handsome man she'd ever seen.

"You built our— A house. Here."

He set his mug on the railing. "I always said I was going to build a house here."

"Yes, you did." She stepped up onto the deck and

walked past him to the railing. "It's still as beautiful as it ever was."

White foam rolled over the rocks at the river's curve. She braced her shoulders and forced herself to look at the rushing water curling over the rocks.

"Why?" she asked.

The question was simple. Why had he built this home, here, where they'd sat on the grass and dreamed young dreams together. Turning to him, she searched his guarded eyes.

"I built this house here because it wasn't just *our* dream, it was also *my* dream, Jolie. Just because you left didn't mean I had to stop dreaming. I wanted a house here on this spot and so I built it."

She crossed her arms, a conscious effort to shut out the pain this confrontation was causing. Was pain the only thing they had left to give each other?

"Y-you did a good job," she admitted, studying the house's lines. "It's a beautiful place."

He looked at a loss for words at her admission. "Thanks," he said curtly. "So why are you here?"

"I came to see the bend. To think…about things."

"You didn't know my home was here?"

She shook her head.

"It's a good place to think. That's what I do best out here."

Her stomach felt like it was turning upside down doing airscrews, which used to be her favorite kayak trick. She knew it was time to just lay her cards out on the table and come clean. "Morgan, I wish you'd give us a second chance."

"There is no us anymore."

Fire flamed inside of her. "You wouldn't know it from that kiss—"

"Not fair, Jolie. That was a mistake."

"I think you're afraid of us. I think you're just as afraid of letting me back in as I am of getting back in that water."

She expected him to deny it. He didn't.

"Maybe." His eyes were hard and as dark as a moonless night sky. "We've been over this."

"No. We've been over the fact that you won't let me teach here because you think I need to go back to competing. What we haven't been over is that you won't open your heart to me and admit that you still love me."

She held her breath. Of all the brazen assumptions to make, she knew this could be the most presumptuous. When he said nothing, she somehow found the strength to continue.

"You think it's so easy to tell me to get back in that kayak and do what I love, yet you won't risk—"

"I don't have to risk anything, Jolie. I'm fine the way I am. You're not."

"You don't know what I am."

"Jolie, I've told you before and I'll tell you again. I will not give you a place to hide."

She started to tell him it wasn't his responsibility either way, that if she wanted to quit kayaking, that was her choice. But she couldn't have that conversation with him again—she just couldn't.

"Have you told the boys you won't be coming back?" he asked. "They need to know, and it needs to come from you."

"No, I haven't. I was hoping…" One look in his eyes told her there was no point in finishing that sentence.

"I'm not renewing your contract and that's final."

She stared at this man she loved, this man she didn't understand. That was that; it was done. She'd done everything except beg and she wouldn't do that. Not that it would have done any good anyway.

"I'll tell them, Morgan." She turned and walked to the steps.

"I do love you, Jolie. Always have, always will. There just is no *us* anymore. You don't get to always make the rules. You don't get to just walk out when you want and then walk back in when you want."

She glanced over her shoulder, wishing—regretting. "You're right," she managed, then walked down the steps. What more was there to say other than asking if he'd ever thought about forgiving her—but he'd probably thought of that and rejected it. Asking him would feel like begging, and she just couldn't do it.

It was time to move on—yes, time to figure out a plan for her life and move forward.

This was over.

Morgan was elbow-deep in paperwork when Randolph walked into his office the next morning and laid a form on the desk.

"Jolie's official application."

"I told her I'd never hire her."

"She told me that when she dropped it off at the house yesterday morning. She said she still wanted to make it formal. She wants this application in her file."

"Why?" Morgan rubbed the bridge of his nose. She'd dropped the application off before she'd ridden out and discovered the house. And him. Before they'd talked yesterday evening. "I won't change my mind."

Exasperation lined his dad's brow. "I know you were hurt, son. I guess I can admit that after watching the two of you together these last few months, I'd hoped there might be a chance for reconciliation. But that won't happen if you aren't willing to take a chance. Son, let go of your pride if you love her and fight for this relationship."

Morgan pushed back from his desk and stood. "Do you think watching her go again is easy? Because it isn't. Dad, the *easiest* thing I could do would be to sign a new contract and let her stay. But I won't do that."

"Morgan, when your mother died, I didn't have a choice but to let the Lord have her. And I'll admit I was angry about that. Some people in this life get miracles—we didn't when it came to your mother. And when Jolie left you, it was one more time in your life when you didn't get the miracle. I hated that, son. But this time, you're getting the chance to have it. Now you just have to take it."

Morgan glared at his dad. "No." He couldn't be more plain than that.

"Then you may lose her forever. Are you really prepared for that? I think in the back of your mind you hoped she'd come back some day. That's why you built that house where you did, and that's why you haven't moved on and found someone else."

"What ever happened to 'when you love someone, let them go'?" His jaw jerked as he spat out the question.

His dad looked sad. "'If they love you, they'll return,'" Randolph said, finishing the quote for him. "What do you think is happening here, Morg?"

"The boys are going to need support after today," Morgan said, closing the door on the topic of him and Jolie, and moving on to what counted. "She's telling them she's leaving."

"They're resilient. They'll survive. It will be hard, though. They've bonded with Jolie like nothing I've ever seen."

"And that was what I was afraid of all along."

His dad pinned him with sharp eyes. "Morgan, you're harder than even I realized." Randolph turned and left Morgan to himself.

It had been all he could do not to go after Jolie yesterday when she'd left his home, telling himself one more time that this was for the best. If he gave her any kind of encouragement, she'd stay. And he would always be afraid—yes, he admitted to himself that he was afraid—that she would regret walking away from kayaking.

His dad believed Jolie coming home was a miracle, that all Morgan had to do was reach out and accept it. But Morgan was more afraid of seeing regret in her eyes down the road if she stayed.

And he was more afraid of that than losing her.

Miracle or no miracle, Jolie regretting coming back to him was the one thing he couldn't live with.

Chapter Twenty

Jolie knew it was time to tell the boys that she wouldn't be around next year. They needed time to adjust to the idea. And so did she.

So the last thing she was expecting was to walk into a classroom decorated for a party. There was a large sign that said "We love you, Jolie!" covering the projection screen. Colored ribbons from the storeroom dangled from the ceiling fans, whipping around as the two fans turned.

"Surprise!" the boys yelled when she entered, all smiles as they surrounded her.

"What's all this?" she asked, her hand on her heart as she looked around at her classroom. It was a sight she'd never forget.

The smaller boys were all talking excitedly. "Hold on, buckaroos," Joseph said, laughing as he calmed them down. When they quieted, he grinned his lopsided smile. "We wanted to make sure you knew how much we appreciate you being here, coming on at the last minute to take on a bunch of ragtags like us. You didn't have to do it but you did."

"Yeah," Wes said, looking a little worried. "It's good to be appreciated. We just wanted you to know."

Jolie bit her lip, tears brimming in her eyes. She sucked in a hard breath. "Thanks," she croaked like a frog. "You have no idea what this means to me."

That had all the boys beaming. They looked so proud that her heart clutched in her chest and she had to close her eyes.

"This is the sweetest thing anyone has ever done for me. And I mean that. And you are not ragtags. You are the kind of kids a woman could call her own—and I do. I want you to know that."

Their smiles faded, and she knew they could hear the sadness in her voice.

"I need you to sit down. I have to tell you something."

"Not that you're going to leave," Sammy blurted out, panic in his eyes.

Jolie hated this. He'd recently lost his family and now he'd formed an attachment to her and *she* was leaving. What would that do to him?

"Yes, I am. I have to. I'm sorry. Listen, Sammy, everyone, there are just some things that can't be changed. But my leaving has nothing to do with all of you. I have loved every minute of my time here since the first day I hopped out of my Jeep and saw you standing there. I love all of you."

Wes and Joseph looked down at the floor, not meeting her gaze.

Dear Lord, help me.

"If you loved us, you would stay." Sammy's brown eyes held unshed tears, his chin trembled and his voice was a faint whisper.

Jolie went to her knees in front of him. "I can't stay."

"Why not?"

How could she tell them Morgan hadn't renewed her contract? They would resent him, and that would be terrible because they had to have a good relationship with him. She had to preserve that no matter what.

What Morgan was doing, he was doing out of a misplaced concern. At least that was the assumption that was getting her through this.

Morgan was trying to do what was right for her.

The realization slammed into her as she looked into Sammy's dear face. This wasn't about not forgiving her...it was about doing what he believed was right. Jolie's heart raced at the realization.

Trying to grasp this new information she continued, "This was always a temporary position. You knew that, Sammy. All of you did. As much as I love being here, I have commitments that I have to keep."

And it was true, she did. Morgan had been right about that.

But you can come back...?

The words whispered through her. She heard a horn honk outside and she smiled. "It's going to be all right, guys. I promise. Sammy, it will be okay. Don't be afraid. Okay?"

He nodded. "Okay."

She hugged him tightly, then stood. "I didn't know y'all were fixin' things up for a party—it goes to show you great minds think alike because I was planning on having one myself. If I'm right, that horn is Ms. Jo and Mabel out there with a truckload of homemade pies. I ordered them for an end-of-term celebration."

"Awesome." Wes jumped up and headed to the door. "I'll help bring them in."

Jolie chuckled. "Y'all have worked so hard, you deserve it."

Ms. Jo's pies could make anyone smile, and she sure hoped it was true today as she watched the kids race outside to help, including Sammy after she'd urged him.

Glancing around the decorated room filled her with determination. No way could she just walk away. There had to be another alternative. And she planned to find it.

"What do you mean you can't do anything about it?" Ms. Jo demanded a few hours later after Jolie let the kids head out early for the day. She'd managed to turn the day around somewhat, though Sammy had remained quiet. He'd participated but kept asking her questions that told her he was still worrying. She just prayed that time would help.

"Yes, who does Morgan think he is making you leave if you don't want to?" Mabel snorted.

"I tell you what, I was miffed at you for what you did to him, but now I'm equally miffed at Morgan. That man needs a knock upside the head, if you ask me."

"Whoa, there, aren't you two the ones who were telling me not to get any ideas? To just be friends?"

"Well," Ms. Jo snapped, "what else were we supposed to say? We didn't want him to get hurt any more than he already had been. We were just trying to be cautious."

"That being said," Mabel added, swiping another forkful of leftover coconut pie, "I agree with Jo. Who is he to tell you you have to leave?"

"He's the guy holding the teaching contract."

Ms. Jo and Mabel gaped at her.

"What?" she asked, bewildered.

Ms. Jo glared at her with impatience. "Who says just because you don't work at Sunrise that you have to leave Dew Drop?"

The door crashed open before Jolie fully processed

Ms. Jo's declaration, and Caleb rushed into the room. "Jolie, come quick. We can't find Sammy. He ran away!"

Some of the boys had stopped by the office and told Morgan Sammy was missing, so he was already on the phone with Tucker when Jolie and Caleb came racing out of the schoolhouse, Ms. Jo and Mabel hotfooting it behind them. They all hurried toward him across the pasture.

Tucker had told him that he'd be there in a few minutes. Morgan had never been happier that his big brother was the sheriff of Dew Drop County. And Rowdy and Chet were on their way with their group, too.

"Caleb said there was a note," Jolie gasped, grabbing his arm as she arrived.

He handed her the note, and his gut clenched watching Jolie, her eyes glistening while she read the words Sammy had painstakingly printed out on a piece of white notebook paper.

Jolie, I'm going to make you proud enough of me that you won't leave.

"What does this mean?" She blinked hard, fighting off tears.

"I'm not sure. He's got a plan, it sounds like. We'll find him," Morgan assured her. "Tucker and Rowdy and the men are on the way. Dad, Pepper, Wes and Joseph are already out there on the roads leading out from the ranch."

She bit her lip. "Okay. We'll find him," she said as if to herself.

Clare and John, Sammy's house parents, hurried from the chow hall with Nana, clearly worried.

"He's crazy about you," Clare said, squeezing Jolie's arm. "He's just come alive since you showed up. Well, all the boys have, actually. They were devastated that you're leaving. But this…" Her words trailed off and she dabbed at tears.

"Leaving, that's the stupidest thing I've ever heard," Ms. Jo snapped, shooting Morgan a stern look as she and Mabel joined Nana in giving Clare some comfort.

Morgan tried not to think about his part in this—not right now. Now he had to hold everyone together and find Sammy. His gaze locked on Jolie. "We'll get a search up once Tucker gets here. We'll find him," Morgan told her again, wanting to give her a hug and ease the alarm in her eyes. But Jolie crossed her arms and nodded once, as if to block him out.

He couldn't say he blamed her.

Jolie fought to stay in control as the sound of Tucker's siren in the far-off distance signaled they would soon be taking action. But it wasn't happening fast enough for her. She needed to do something soon or she'd go crazy.

"Caleb," she said. "Who was the last to see Sammy?"

"Me. We were going to play in the hay barn, but he said he had to do something, so I went with Tony instead. We decided to go see what he was doing and found the note on his bed."

Tony piped in. "We took it down to Ms. Clare right when we found it."

"Do you guys have any idea where he might have gone?"

They all shook their heads. Jolie felt helpless as Tucker's SUV pulled into the yard and came to a quick halt. Turning off the lights and siren, he stepped from the vehicle and strode their way. Even though his aviation shades hid his eyes, the hard set of his jaw said he was taking this seriously.

"Tucker, glad you're here," Morgan said, looking just as grim as his brother.

"Any word?" Tucker asked, pulling his shades off, looking from Morgan to Jolie.

"None so far," Morgan answered.

Jolie wrapped her arms around herself. "Tucker, if he's walking off the property, the guys would have found him by now. A little kid like him couldn't have gotten far on foot in less than an hour."

"True. We'll start searching the ranch. But we need some facts first."

"These three were the last to see him." Morgan placed an arm around Caleb's shoulders. Jolie found herself wishing his arm were around her instead. "They came straight to us when they found the note."

"Do you have it?"

"I do." Jolie thrust it at him, anxious for his trained eye to see it. She watched as he read it, meeting Morgan's gaze for a brief moment. "Any hints in there that we're missing?"

"Sounds like he has something to prove. Any thoughts about that?"

"He's been better about being scared," Caleb said.

Just then, Randolph drove up with Joseph and Wes from scouting the roads. Randolph shook his head as he strode toward the crowd. He, Morgan and Tucker went off and had a discussion, and Nana came and put her arm around Jolie.

Within minutes cars began to arrive full of folks from town, like Chili and Drewbaker. Walter Pepper and the other ranch hands came soon after, having had no luck searching the immediate area. More law enforcement with a team of search dogs was on the way. Within the hour they had a full-blown search going.

Jolie had been going over her conversation with Sammy from that morning, and the note he'd left. Her gut was trying to tell her something…he'd asked her where she was trying to kayak and she'd told him about the trail behind her house that led down to the river where she had been going to picture herself getting in the water. She'd confessed that she hadn't been able to get in so far though. Surely he wasn't trying to prove—Jolie halted in her tracks.

Proud enough of me that you won't leave.

Spinning around Jolie searched for Morgan. He was getting on his horse on the other side of the pasture, about to start a mounted search. Racing toward him, Jolie had never been so happy to be in shape in all of her life. He spotted her and rode out to meet her.

"What's up, Jolie?" he asked as he brought his horse to a halt.

"I think he might be at the river behind my house. I think he's going to kayak."

"Seriously?"

Jolie nodded. "He wants to make me proud. Maybe he thinks if he can do what I can't, I won't leave."

Morgan's brows knitted beneath his straw Stetson. He held a hand out to her and pulled his boot from the stirrup. "Come on, let's go check it out."

Jolie didn't waste time. She reached for his hand, rammed her boot in the stirrup and let him hoist her up behind him. They were heading toward her house almost before she got her arms around his waist. Jolie clung to Morgan, her heart racing with hope as they galloped across the pasture.

"You sure you can face this? Do I need to get someone else to help me?" he asked over his shoulder.

"I'll handle it," she said with no hesitation. If they

found Sammy in that river current—she prayed he hadn't done such a foolish thing, but if he had—he would need her. "I'm the best person for this."

"That's my girl," Morgan said. His words dug deep—it had been a long time since she'd been his girl. A long, long time.

Too long.

This wasn't the time to think about the past between them, but as they rode, memories crowded in alongside the worry for Sammy. Like a kaleidoscope of past, present and a future yet untold, everything shifted in and out of focus, bringing new images to her mind's eye.

When they made it to the cabin, Jolie's heart stopped as she looked at the spot where her kayaks sat. "My yellow kayak is missing," she said grimly. "He's out there, Morgan."

"Looks that way," Morgan said.

"I need to grab my gear." She jumped from the horse, raced inside the house and grabbed her backpack from where it rested in the corner, forgotten. Inside it was her kayaking gear, and her rescue ropes. Outside again, she went straight for one of her other kayaks, hoisted it to her shoulder and without waiting for Morgan she hurried to her Jeep and stowed it across the backseat, not bothering to attach it to the roof rack.

Morgan helped straighten it and then hopped in as she cranked the key and rammed the gearshift. "Hang on," she warned, and punched the gas. Wheeling through the backyard and onto the faint trail, she cut through to the clearing.

When they hit the steep hill, the Jeep's wheels left land for a moment as they surged forward, soared through the air and hit hard before racing downhill.

They didn't say much as they scanned the land while

they drove, hoping to find Sammy before he made it to the water.

How long had he been gone?

When they made it to the trail that led to the water, Jolie jerked the Jeep to a halt and grabbed her kayak.

"I can carry that for you," Morgan offered.

She shook her head. "I always carry my own load."

It was part of the sport—her kayak was as much a part of her as her arms. "It's okay," she assured Morgan over her shoulder. "Thanks for the offer."

She jogged down the path where she'd had her meltdown that day that had ended in the kiss she couldn't forget. Morgan didn't ask her if she was all right again—he just jogged beside her and kept up. They topped the hill, bending down to miss a couple of low-slung tree limbs. She could hear the river now, the rush of rapids downstream from where they would put in. It was an ominous sound to Jolie. Her heartbeat became erratic and her skin clammy.

Thinking of Sammy, she never slowed down, refusing to give in. She was going in if Sammy needed her. No question about it.

Bursting through the last of the trees she headed straight down the embankment, scanning the water anxiously. And praying hard.

Her heart stopped. "There!" she shouted, spotting him on the far side of the river clinging to a tree branch, just past the first set of rapids.

Instead of holding him under, the vortex had spat him out when he'd slipped out of his kayak. She thanked God for that.

And for giving her a window of opportunity to get to him.

But there was no way to get down the rocks to Sammy. Going through the rapids was the only way.

She'd have to hold the kayak in control while maneuvering to him. And once she had him, they'd have to make it through the worst rapids together in a one-man kayak.

"You can do this, Jolie." Morgan's penetrating eyes told her he had faith in her. Even having seen what a basket case she'd been, he had faith.

Her head was swimming. "You better get downstream and be ready in case you have to grab him," she advised as she started moving again. Morgan would know the spot she meant—it would be his only shot to grab Sammy if she missed, or if Sammy lost his grip on the tree before she got to him. If they both missed, the river would sweep him into the worst section of the rapids. His only chance then would be in God's hands.

Jolie prayed.

Glancing over her shoulder she saw Morgan racing down the path. He'd be standing between two large rocks in a shallow section that had a slippery fast current, just bypassing a pool of calm water to the right, perfect for a takeout.

At the water's edge, Jolie fought her demons, thinking only of Sammy. She was in the kayak within seconds—no hesitation, paddle in hand and moving. She found her line in the water quickly and set herself up to hit the rapid perfectly. She took the first set with no problem, a warm-up for what was to come.

Keeping her line, she set herself up for the second set of rapids, this one was the money spot, as they called it in competition, the one that counted…

This one's for Sammy.

The water was cold as it washed over her, the current

swift, strong from the rain they'd had up north two days earlier. She prayed God would keep Sammy's strength up, and thanked Him for giving her the ability to do what needed to be done to save him.

She took the rapid, a mad vortex of powerful, churning water with the means to pull a person down and not spit her out until it felt like it. She wished for her yellow banana—her old friend—but this kayak would have to do.

She cut through the rocks with skill honed from hard work and God's gift…and then she maneuvered a perfect roll, dipping head-first beneath the surface then rolling out and flipping the kayak into the air. The move required strength as she twisted her body, forcing the kayak to alter its course. She landed it perfectly and with a swift push of her paddle was right next to Sammy beneath the tree.

Jolie held the boat still with the paddle against the rocks behind him. She reached with her free arm, muscles burning from the effort, and she got him. His eyes were huge, glazed with fear, his lips purple from the chill.

"Y-you came for me," he gasped, clinging to the limb.

"I'll *always* come for you," she declared, voice hoarse with emotion, knowing it was true. "Let go of the tree," she urged against the roar of the water. Thankfully, Sammy was thinking clearly enough to respond with a nod and do as he was asked. He took her hand and she pulled him toward the boat. It was hard to do, since she was having to use the paddle to hold the boat steady and keep them out of the current. If she wasn't careful she could be swept away from him. "You have to climb up by yourself, Sammy, okay? I can hold you steady, but you have to climb on your own."

There was no place for him except on top of the kayak in front of her, with his feet on the stern. This wasn't a normal situation—it was a tricky balancing act. God's hand and His alone steadied the boat as she held off the current with one hand on the paddle. She felt her strength waning—she knew she wasn't going to last much longer.

"When you get up, lean back against me, hold on to the deck line and keep your feet on the kayak in front of you. Can you do that?"

"Y-yes, I can." Even though his teeth were chattering, there was power in his voice now. Jolie was so proud of Sammy as he scrambled up the kayak and eased into place.

"We're going to make it," she told him as he leaned against her. "Hold on, buddy, here we go," she said, and let the current have them, sweeping them back into the dangerous flow.

Chapter Twenty-One

Morgan prayed harder than he ever had in his whole life as he watched the rescue. Jolie was amazing—her strength and skill awed him as she held it all together and came through the last set of rapids with Sammy in front of her. Once it was clear they'd make the trip without flipping, he moved to the calm pool where he knew she was headed.

Morgan steadied the kayak, then took Sammy into his arms. The boy looked slightly dazed as Morgan hugged him hard, thanking God. "You're okay, little man," he said, looking into his tense face. Limp as a rag, Sammy nodded and rested his head against Morgan's heart. Jolie climbed from her kayak, her exhaustion evident in the way she moved.

"We need to get him to a doctor," she said, hoisting her kayak to the shore and leaving it behind as she assisted Morgan in getting Sammy up the steep incline to the path.

"I got them on my cell. An ambulance should be getting to the woods' edge soon."

Hurrying along the path, Morgan kept talking to Sammy as Jolie held branches out of their way. Sammy looked up at him, his eyes bright with tears. "I didn't mean to mess up. I tried to make y'all proud of me. I tried to make Jolie see that I could help her in the water so she would stay. You won't send me away now, will you?"

Morgan held him closer, and kept his pace. "Never. You're going to be fine, Sammy. We're not sending you anywhere—you are part of our family."

Jolie placed her hand on Sammy's head as they continued to hurry along the path. "I was scared for you, Sammy, but God kept you safe out there today. You're going to be all right. I'm crazy about you, don't you know that?"

And Morgan was crazy about *her.* Hearing her say those words to Sammy made his heart stop in his chest. It was going to be almost impossible to let her go.

She'd proven she could get back in the water, and she could do it with style. Jolie belonged out there—it was evident to anyone who saw her in action. After today, he had no doubt.

Sammy obviously didn't want to see her go any more than Morgan did.

But they would have to let her.

They were just coming out of the woods when the emergency vehicles came across the pasture with Tucker in the lead. It was like the cavalry was coming. Morgan had never been happier to see his brother in all his life.

Sammy had been through a harrowing experience and it was a miracle he'd survived long enough for Jolie to get to him. It was God who had held Sammy to that tree, no doubt about it. And it was God who was going to have to give Sammy—and Morgan—the strength to see her leave.

A few hours later, Jolie held a cup of coffee in her hands, letting the warmth sink into her bones. She wasn't sure the chill would ever leave her. Sitting on a bench on the porch of the chow hall, she watched the boys laughing and playing a game of football in the yard. Morgan and his dad and brothers were sitting together at the picnic table, talking to various people from town who'd come out to help with the rescue and then stayed to celebrate. Sammy sat on the bench between Morgan and Tucker, looking a little stunned that so many people had come to make sure he was safe.

Nana, Ms. Jo and Mabel were hustling around making sure everyone had something to eat and drink. Everyone was so relieved that Sammy was safe that the rescue party had turned into a regular party.

Jolie's role as the hero was making her uncomfortable. She'd had to repeat to Tucker what she'd done, then defer to Morgan. Morgan had a version of the tale that was so full of praise she couldn't listen, but his version pleased everyone more than her clinical retelling of events had.

"I gotta say one thing," Edwina said, stopping beside Jolie, topping off her cup of coffee without bothering to ask. "You got some nerves of steel, Jolie. You done good savin' that boy. You know I ain't never made it no secret that I ain't got a lick of use for men. But Morgan's got himself some good qualities aside from bein' drop-dead gorgeous—yeah, I do have eyes." She gave Jolie a grin. "But truly, you could do a whole lot worse—believe me, if you were to meet Lester or Darin or even Marv—any of that bunch of losers I married—you'd have a clue how much worse it could *get*."

Jolie smiled, chuckling. Edwina had not been lucky in love.

"There you go. If my love life won't pull a chuckle out of you, nothing will. But honestly, maybe you need to rethink this leavin' thing. If that man looked at me the way he looks at you, I might be tempted to dip my toe back into the matrimonial waters. Somethin' to think about." She winked and was gone, off to spread her cheer elsewhere.

If she only knew that this time, it wasn't Jolie who'd chosen a different life. It was Morgan.

Jolie looked over at Sammy, who had stayed away from her since they'd made it back to the ranch, sticking close to Morgan's side. It was as if he needed to shut her out.

And she hated it.

But there was a huge positive here—Sammy had come so far. He wasn't lying anymore, and he'd taken a risk today. However misguided his actions had been, he'd left his fears behind and tried to be strong. Jolie knew she'd had a part in his growth. Looking at him now, she was filled with pride of accomplishment like nothing she'd ever felt on the river.

Jolie had no doubts now about what she was going to do with the rest of her life. What she didn't know was how Morgan was going to handle it.

He thought he'd figured out the rest of her life for her.

But he was wrong.

Standing, she dropped the blanket on the bench and walked over to where he sat. "Morgan, may I speak to you?"

When he looked up at her and saw her serious expression, elation slid off his face and his eyes darkened.

"Sure."

Jolie led them away from the crowd, to the quiet of the stables. The smell of hay and feed greeted her, and from the cool shadows she heard the soft nicker of newborn colts. She slowly turned and faced an unsmiling Morgan.

"I'm staying, Morgan. I'm retiring from competition,"

she said quietly. "I know where you stand on all this, but I know what I want, and I know what's best for me."

"Jolie, I saw you out there today. You were magnificent. To leave that beauty and skill behind would be a waste. You are meant for great things."

She smiled. "Yes, I am. And so are you. Here on this ranch is where the great things happen. Watching these boys flourish, and loving them. This is the great thing I'm meant for now. This is what I choose." She studied his face as he stared down at her. "I'd like your blessing, Morgan, but I don't need it. My plan is to move to Dew Drop and get a teaching job at the public school, and volunteer on the ranch, if you'll have me."

Morgan had grown still. His jaw jerked and his eyes cut through her, searching for the truth. "I don't know what to say," he said. "I know for me the boys are enough. At least, it satisfies me. But you're going to regret—"

"I already regret, Morgan. I regret leaving you. I regret hurting you. Yet I know that God had a plan back then and it was meant to be. And now I know *this* is meant to be. So I'm here to stay, and I'm praying that at some point you will trust my love for you and let me into your heart again."

She stepped close to him and placed her hand on his heart. It was racing.

"I love you, Morgan McDermott, and you love me. You told me so. Can you let me back into your life?"

He didn't say anything, and her heart sank. She'd hoped if he knew she wasn't leaving it would change his mind. But as she stepped away from him, she knew her plan wasn't going to change one bit. Dew Drop was where she was supposed to be.

"I hope one day you'll be able to accept my being

here, Morgan, and even let me help out with the boys. It would mean a lot to me." Jolie turned, not knowing what else to say. She'd made it to the double doors of the stable when his hand on her arm halted her.

"Jolie."

She faced him, framed in the doorway with the soft breeze in her hair. She knew she must look a sight after all they'd been through on the water, but she didn't care.

"Don't you know it would be easy to agree? The hard part is to let you go. I hope you understand that."

She lifted her hand to cup his strong jaw. "I do," she whispered, nodding. "I truly do. But this is where I *want* to be. Where I need to be. With you. And the boys. And no regrets. None."

She could see the war in his eyes, his beautiful, deep, fathomless eyes. His forehead crinkled and his jaw tensed as he struggled with the right thing to do. The right thing to do by *her*.

"You have to trust that what I say is true, Morgan. I love you, and if you open your heart to me I will never, ever leave you. Please trust me."

He nodded ever so slightly. His eyes calmed and a slow smile eased across his face as he turned his head to kiss her palm. His hand came up and took hers, and Jolie's heart cracked open with love. And hope.

No words were needed as his arms came around her and his lips met hers. "I love you, Jolie Sheridan. Will you marry me?" he whispered.

With tears in her eyes, she nodded. And behind them, whoops, cheers and clapping erupted.

"Well—" Morgan chuckled "—it's a done deal now. You're stuck with us. Because I'm not telling *them* any different."

Jolie looked across the grass to her boys. "Good. This is my *family,* and I'm not going anywhere."

Squeezing her hand tightly in his, Morgan looked at her with love in his eyes. "Then let's go make it official."

She smiled, her heart in full bloom. "Lead the way, cowboy. Lead the way."

Epilogue

"*Hubba, hubba,* come to papa," Wes croaked from the front pew where all sixteen boys were standing in the church.

Morgan would have gone over and thumped him on the ear if he hadn't been standing beside the preacher and thinking a more polite version of the same thing as Jolie entered the sanctuary on the arm of her dad. She was so beautiful that he could do nothing but hold her gaze and watch her walk down the aisle toward him. He'd been waiting six long years for this day.

After she'd convinced him that she wanted a life on the ranch with him and the boys, they'd wasted no time setting the date. Jolie had wanted to get married immediately, but they'd given themselves a month.

It was a cold day in January, with a fine layer of snow on the ground and the wind rattling the church windows. He'd hoped for a sunny day for Jolie, but she'd said even a blizzard wouldn't keep her from becoming Mrs. Morgan McDermott.

For Morgan, the sun had come out the moment Jolie

said yes. He'd gotten down on his knees in front of the boys so they could see how it should be done. She'd laughingly agreed, and her laughter had filled every space in his heart.

He thanked God for bringing her back to him in *His* time. Morgan recognized that Jolie had needed the time away, and even though he wasn't real high on thinkin' it, he'd needed the time she was away, too. Although he'd loved her, he'd tried to corral her when what she'd needed was space to find her way and become her own person.

Now she could live life with him on the ranch with her whole heart and no regrets.

"She looks like a fairy princess," B.J. whispered so loudly the whole church heard him.

Morgan had to agree. To get a good view of her coming up the aisle, the two boys had moved over to peek around Wes, who was standing on the end.

Her long, white dress was soft and kind of sparkly as it moved about her. She practically looked like she was floating. Her eyes were shining with happiness and locked to his as the space slowly disappeared between them. Her lips trembled with a soft smile.

"She *is* a fairy princess," Sammy said, puffing his chest out. "She's ours and she's here to stay."

Joseph had moved up behind them. "Yes, she is, boys," he said quietly. "Now let's move on back to our seats and let the preacher marry her up with Morgan."

Beside Morgan, his best men—Rowdy and Tucker—chuckled.

"That'd be a good idea," Rowdy murmured low. "Because Morg here has been waitin' his whole life for this moment."

"You're up next, Rowdy, my man," Morgan heard Tucker tease their little brother.

"Me? Nope, that'd be you, big brother."

Morgan met his dad's steady gaze from the front row and they shared a moment, both thinking it would be interesting to see which one would be next.

The piano drew to a halt as Jolie and her father stopped in front of him.

"Who gives this woman?" the preacher asked.

"Her mother and I," Mr. Sheridan said, and placed Jolie's hand in Morgan's.

Jolie smiled that hundred-watts-of-pure-joy smile of hers, aiming it straight at him as she squeezed his hand, their eyes locked on each other. "I love you," she whispered, and as one they turned toward the preacher.

"This is gonna be *goooood,*" Sammy whispered.

"It already is," Caleb hissed.

"We got her for always now," B.J. said, his voice loud and clear, making the congregation chuckle.

Jolie turned and shared that killer smile of hers with the boys. "And I've got y'all," she assured them.

Morgan chuckled and cleared his throat. "Preacher, the floor is officially yours. Let's get rollin' so I can put a ring on her finger."

"At last," Rowdy said with a chuckle.

Morgan shot him a warning look—he hadn't forgotten that payback was owed to his little brother. And he was a patient man.

Jolie turned back to the preacher and nodded. "Okay," she said. "Make me the happiest woman in the world."

"Finally," Morgan grunted. Laughter rumbled behind them as the preacher proceeded to make Morgan the happiest man in the world. At last.

* * * * *

If you enjoyed this story by Debra Clopton,
be sure to look for the other Love Inspired books
out this month!

Dear Reader,

Thank you for joining me at Sunrise Ranch deep in the heart of West Texas. I have to say that I loved creating this new bunch of characters. As you can tell from reading this book, I wanted to keep you on your toes with them, so that you'll never know what to expect when you visit the ranch or the small town of Dew Drop and the Spotted Cow Café.

Just like my Mule Hollow series, I love never knowing what my characters are going to do next. So I'm busy working on the second story and having fun seeing what mischief everyone is getting into…stay tuned!

I so enjoyed telling Morgan and Jolie's story, and I hope you are looking forward to watching the other two McDermott brothers meet their matches later in the year.

The theme verse of this book, John 14:18, is one of my favorite of God's promises: I will not leave you comfortless—I will come to you.

I loved using the theme of comfort in this book. Sammy needed comfort, and Jolie and Morgan were there for him, helping him through his grief. Jolie needed comforting, and so did Morgan. For all of them, God was the ultimate comforter, and He put them all in place to comfort each other.

I pray that if you need comfort today, you'll bow your head and talk it over with God. He is there to comfort you, too.

Until next time, live, laugh and seek God with all your hearts!

Debra Clopton

Questions for Discussion

1. Morgan's mother's vision for creating the foster program at Sunrise Ranch was to share the beauty and blessing of this West Texas ranch with less fortunate boys who had no place to call home. How did Morgan feel about his mother's dream? What are his plans for the future?

2. Why did Randolph McDermott hire Jolie Sheridan when she'd hurt his son, Morgan, so badly?

3. Despite what he is feeling when he learns what his father has done, Morgan is determined to be a good role model for the boys of the ranch. What does this say about him as a man?

4. Why do the boys of the ranch react in such a heartfelt and wistful manner when they watch the mother horse care for her newborn?

5. Jolie has regrets despite the fabulous life she has lived and the adventure and success she has known. She is torn between two worlds—the one she chose and the one she left behind. Have you ever felt torn between two choices? Did you pray for God's guidance in making the right choice?

6. How do Ms. Jo and Mabel react to Jolie's return to town? They love Jolie and Morgan and are not even thinking of matchmaking. Why?

7. Sammy is certain his family is going to come back

and get him. Even in his time of need and distress, when his parents abandoned him, God was taking care of Sammy. What did God do for Sammy?

8. Putting his personal reasons for not wanting Jolie at the ranch aside, what is the main reason Morgan thinks her teaching the boys is a bad idea?

9. Jolie realizes, as she and Morgan have their first battle of wills outside the classroom under the oak tree, that God has given her a purpose in coming back to the ranch. She realizes she can help the boys. How does this make her feel?

10. When Morgan realizes he still loves Jolie and that she is afraid of the water, what is his reaction? What does he contemplate doing? Are you glad that he makes the choice to help her? Why?

11. Jolie is terrified of the water, and the nightmares haunt her. She is struggling and asking God to help her, but it isn't an overnight fix. Sometimes in order for God to help us, it takes time. Have you ever had to have patience while you waited for God to act?

12. When Sammy needs her, does Jolie hesitate? What does she do?

13. Why is helping Jolie get back into the water an act of love and sacrifice on Morgan's part?

14. Jolie is forced to take a stand when it comes to choosing to leave or stay. What does she realize

when she has to make the choice on her own without Morgan's help?

15. Sammy thought if he was good, Jolie would stay. Like Morgan knew in the beginning of the book, he needed stability and commitment in his life, as did all the boys. When Jolie makes up her mind to stay, it's about more than her love for Morgan. It's about finding her purpose in life—what is that? Sometimes it takes a while to realize our purpose. Do you believe that God has a purpose for each of us? Have you asked God to help you find your purpose?

COMING NEXT MONTH from Love Inspired®

AVAILABLE MAY 21, 2013

PLAIN ADMIRER

Brides of Amish Country

Patricia Davids

Joann Yoder lost her dream home when the boss's nephew took her job. Only her secret pen pal understands her feelings. What'll happen when she discovers he is her Plain admirer?

SEASIDE BLESSINGS

Starfish Bay

Irene Hannon

When Kristen Andrews is unexpectedly reunited with the daughter she gave up for adoption, her tough-on-the-outside new landlord can't help being pulled into her life....

THE FIREMAN'S HOMECOMING

Gordon Falls

Allie Pleiter

Clark's and Melba's pasts are tangled by a family secret. Can they find the grace and love to win a future together?

COURTING HOPE

Jenna Mindel

Trying to move on after a family tragedy, Hope Peterson is shocked to learn that the new minister is the one man she can't forgive...and the only man she's ever loved.

RESTORING HIS HEART

Lorraine Beatty

When she agreed to help the handsome daredevil restore the town landmark he destroyed, Laura Durrant never expected to lose her heart to the man she discovers he is inside.

REUNITED WITH THE SHERIFF

Belle Calhoune

While seeking redemption for past wrongs, Cassidy Blake reconnects with her first love, Sheriff Tate Lynch. But a shocking secret from the past may doom their second chance at love.

SPECIAL EXCERPT FROM

Love Inspired

What happens when opposites attract?

Read on for a sneak peek at SEASIDE BLESSINGS by Irene Hannon, available June 2013 from Love Inspired.

Clint Nolan padded barefoot toward the front of the house as the doorbell gave an impatient peal. After spending the past hour fighting a stubborn tree root on the nature trail at The Point, he wanted food, not visitors.

Forcibly changing his scowl to the semblance of a smile, he unlocked the door, pulled it open—and froze.

It was her.

Miss Reckless-Driver. Kristen Andrews.

And she didn't look any too happy to see him.

His smile morphed back to a scowl.

Several seconds of silence ticked by.

Finally he spoke. "Can I help you?" The question came out cool and clipped.

She cleared her throat. "I, uh, got your address from the town's bulletin board. Genevieve at the Orchid recommended your place when I, uh, ate dinner there."

Since he'd arrived in town almost three years ago, the sisters at the Orchid had been lamenting his single state. Especially Genevieve.

But the Orchid Café matchmaker was wasting her time. The inn's concierge wasn't the woman for him. No way. Nohow.

And Kristen herself seemed to agree.

"I doubt you'd be interested. It's on the *rustic* side," he said.

LIEXP7818

A spark of indignation sprang to life in her eyes, and her chin rose in a defiant tilt.

Uh-oh. Wrong move.

"Depends on what you mean by rustic. Are you telling me it doesn't have indoor plumbing?"

He folded his arms across his chest. "It has a full bath and a compact kitchen. Very compact."

"How many bedrooms?"

"Two. Plus living room and breakfast nook."

"It's furnished, correct?"

"With the basics."

"I'd like to see it."

Okay. She was no airhead, even if she did spend her days arranging cushy excursions and making dinner reservations for rich hotel guests. But there was an undeniable spark of intelligence—and spunk—in her eyes. She might be uncomfortable around him, but she hadn't liked the implication of his rustic comment one little bit and she was going to make him pay for it. One way or another…

Will Clint and Kristen ever see eye to eye?

Don't miss SEASIDE BLESSINGS by Irene Hannon, on sale June 2013 wherever Love Inspired books are sold!

LIEXP7818